'Don't s[...]weet-heart. I [...] as a delicious [...] than as an appetiser. But one I intend to devour nonetheless.'

'Look, Mr…?'

Narciso raised a brow. 'You're at a masked event, shrouded in secrecy, embroiled in intrigue and mystery, and you want to know my *name*?' he asked cynically.

How could she have forgotten? 'Why do I get the feeling that all this bores you rigid?'

His eyes gleamed. 'How very intuitive of you. You're right, it does. Or it did until I saw you.'

Ruby's heart gave a little kick. One she determinedly ignored. 'You were fully engaged when you played your game. And *that* had nothing to do with me.'

Again that reminder hardened his eyes. 'Ah, but I lost thirty million dollars so I could make what's happening between us happen sooner.'

'There's nothing happening—'

'If you believe *that* then you really are naïve.'

THE 21st CENTURY GENTLEMAN'S CLUB

Where the rich, powerful and passionate come to play!

For years there have been rumours of a secret society where only the richest, the most powerful and the most decadent can embrace their every desire.

Nothing is forbidden in this private world of pleasure.

And when exclusivity is beyond notoriety only those who are invited to join ever know its name…

Q Virtus

Now the truth behind the rumours is about to be revealed!

Find out in:

THE ULTIMATE PLAYBOY
by Maya Blake
July 2014

THE ULTIMATE SEDUCTION
by Dani Collins
August 2014

THE ULTIMATE REVENGE
by Victoria Parker
September 2014

THE ULTIMATE PLAYBOY

BY
MAYA BLAKE

Published in Great Britain 2014
by Mills & Boon, an imprint of Harlequin (UK) Limited,
Eton House, 18-24 Paradise Road, Richmond, Surrey, TW9 1SR

© 2014 Maya Blake

ISBN: 978 0 263 90877 0

Harlequin (UK) Limited's policy is to use papers that are natural,
renewable and recyclable products and made from wood grown in
sustainable forests. The logging and manufacturing processes conform
to the legal environmental regulations of the country of origin.

Printed and bound in Spain
by Blackprint CPI, Barcelona

Maya Blake fell in love with the world of the alpha male and the strong, aspirational heroine when she borrowed her sister's Mills & Boon® at the age of thirteen. Shortly thereafter the dream to plot a happy ending for her own characters was born. Writing for Harlequin® is a dream come true. Maya lives in South East England with her husband and two kids. Reading is an absolute passion, but when she isn't lost in a book she likes to swim, cycle, travel and Tweet!

You can get in touch with her
via e-mail, at mayablake@ymail.com,
or on Twitter: www.twitter.com/mayablake

Recent titles by the same author:

WHAT THE GREEK CAN'T RESIST
WHAT THE GREEK'S MONEY CAN'T BUY
  (The Untamable Greeks)
HIS ULTIMATE PRIZE
MARRIAGE MADE OF SECRETS

Did you know these are also available as eBooks?
Visit www.millsandboon.co.uk

To David and Peter.
Life would be so much duller without you two!

CHAPTER ONE

New York

NARCISO VALENTINO STARED at the box that had been delivered to him. It was large, made with the finest expensive leather, trimmed with velvet rope, with a horseshoe-shaped clasp made of solid twenty-four-carat gold.

Normally, the sight of it brought anticipation and pleasure.

But the ennui that had invited itself for a long-term stay in his life since he'd turned thirty last month leached excitement from him as the stock market leaked money after a juicy disaster.

Lucia had accused him of turning into a boring old man right before her diva exit out of his life two weeks ago.

He allowed himself a little grin of relief. He'd celebrated her departure with a boys' weekend ski trip to Aspen where he'd treated himself to a little palate cleanser in the form of a very enthusiastic Norwegian ski instructor.

But much too quickly, the jaded hollowness had returned.

Rising from his desk, he strode to the window of his seventieth-floor Wall Street office and stared at the New York skyline. Satisfaction eased through him at the thought that he owned a huge chunk of this city.

Money was sexy. Money was power. And The Warlock of Wall Street—as the newspapers had taken to calling him—never denied himself the pull of power and sex.

The opportunity to experience two of his favourite things lay within the package on his desk.

Yet it'd remained unopened for the last hour…

Shrugging off the lethargy, he returned briskly to his desk and flipped the clasp.

The half mask staring up at him from a bed of black satin was exquisite. Pure silver edged with black onyx and Swarovski crystals, its intricate design and flawless detail announced the care and attention that had gone into creating it. Narciso appreciated care and attention. It was what had made him a millionaire by eighteen and a multibillionaire by twenty-five.

His vast wealth was also what had gained him admission into *Q Virtus,* the world's most exclusive gentlemen's club, whose quarterly caucus invitation was the reason for the mask. Two four-inch-long diamond-tipped pins held the mask in place. Pulling them out, he flipped it over to examine the soft, velvet underside, which held the security microchip, his moniker—The Warlock—and the venue, *Q Virtus,* Macau. He ran his thumb over the smooth surface, hoping to summon a little enthusiasm. Failing miserably, he set the mask down and glanced at the second item in the box.

The List.

Zeus, the anonymous head of *Q Virtus,* always provided club members with a discreet list of business interests who would be attending the caucuses. Narciso had chosen not to attend the last two because he'd already dealt with those lists' major players.

His gaze skimmed the heavily embossed paper and his breath caught. Excitement of a different, dangerous kind sizzled through him as the fourth name jumped out at him.

Giacomo Valentino—*Daddy dearest.*

He perused the other names to see if anyone else on the list would make his attendance worthwhile.

His lips twisted. Who the hell was he kidding?

One name and one name only had become *the* deciding factor. There were one or two business interests worth cultivating during the two-day event, but Giacomo was who he intended to interact with.

Although perhaps *interact* was the wrong word.

Setting the list down, he fired up his computer. Entering the security codes, he pulled up the file he kept on his father.

The report his private investigator updated on a regular basis showed that the old man had rallied a little from the blow Narciso had dealt him three months ago.

Rallied but not fully recovered. Within minutes, Narciso was fully up to speed on his father's latest business dealings.

He didn't fool himself into thinking it gave him any sort of upper hand. He knew his father kept a similar file on him. But the game wouldn't have been this interesting if advantages had been one-sided. Nevertheless Narciso gained a lot of satisfaction from knowing he'd won three of their last four skirmishes.

He was contemplating the latest approach to his annihilation campaign when his phone buzzed.

Allowing the distraction, he thumbed the interactive surface and read the message from Nicandro Carvalho, the closest thing he had to a best friend.

Still caught in premature midlife-crisis mode, or are you ready to shake off that clinging BOM image?

Boring old man. A corner of his mouth lifted as his gaze slid to the list and his father's name. Suddenly energised, he whipped back a response.

BOM has left the building. Care to get your ass whopped at poker?

Nicandro's response—Dream on but bring it on—made him laugh for the first time in weeks.

Powering down his laptop, he slammed it shut. His gaze once again fell on the mask. Picking it up, he stashed it in his safe and shrugged into his suit jacket.

Zeus would receive his RSVP in the morning, once he'd devised exactly how he was going to take his father down once and for all.

The internet was a scary place. But it was an invaluable tool if you wanted to hunt down a slippery son of a bitch.

Ruby Trevelli sat cross-legged on her sofa and stared at the blinking cursor awaiting her command. That she was reduced to online trawling for a solution to her problem spiked equal measures of irritation and frustration through her.

She'd made it a point to avoid anything to do with social media. The one time she'd foolishly typed her name into a search engine, the sheer volume of false information she'd discovered had scared her into never trying again.

Of course, she'd also found enough about her parents to have scarred her for life if she hadn't already been scarred.

Tonight, she had no choice. Because despite thousands of pages featuring Narciso Media Corporation, every effort to speak to someone who could help her had been met with a solid stone wall. She'd already wasted a solid hour discovering that a thirty-year-old billionaire named Narciso Valentino owned NMC.

She snorted under her breath. Who on earth named their child *Narciso* anyway? That was like inviting bullies and snark-mongers to feast on the poor child. On the flip side, his unique name had eased her search.

Sucking in a breath, she typed in her next request: *Narciso's New York hangouts.* There were over two million entries. Awesome.

Either there were millions of men out there named Narciso or the man she sought was indecently popular.

Offering up a Hail Mary, she clicked the first link. And nearly gagged at the graphic burlesque images that popped up. *Hell no!*

She closed it and sat back, fighting the rising nausea.

Desperate was fast becoming her middle name but Ruby

refused to accept that the answers to her woeful financial predicament would be found in a skin den.

Biting her inside lip, she exhaled and typed again: *Where's Narciso Valentino tonight?*

Her breath caught as the search engine fired back a quick response. The first linked the domain of a popular tabloid newspaper—one she'd become rudely acquainted with when she'd received her first laptop at ten, logged on and seen her parents splashed over the home page. In the fourteen years since then, she'd avoided the tabloid, just as she avoided her parents nowadays.

Ignoring the ache in her chest, she clicked on the next link that connected to a location app.

For several seconds, she couldn't believe how easily she'd found him. She read the extensive list of celebrities who'd announced their whereabouts freely, including one attending a movie premiere right now in Times Square.

Grabbing the remote, she flipped the TV channel to the entertainment news station, and, sure enough, the movie star was flashing a million-dollar smile at his adoring fans.

She glanced back at the location next to Narciso Valentino's name.

Riga—a Cuban-Mexican nightclub in the Flatiron District in Manhattan.

Glancing at the clock above the TV, she made a quick calculation. If she hurried, she could be there in under an hour. Her heart hammered as she contemplated what she was about to do.

She despised confrontation almost as much as her parents thrived on it. But after weeks of trying to find a solution, she'd reached the end of her tether.

She'd won the NMC reality TV show and scraped together every last cent to come up with her half of the hundred-thousand-dollar capital needed to get her restaurant—Dolce Italia—up and running.

Any help she could've expected from Simon Whittaker, her

ex-business partner and owner of twenty-five per cent of Dolce Italia, was now a thing of the past.

She clenched her fist as she recalled their last confrontation.

Finding out that the man she'd developed feelings for was married with a baby on the way had been shock enough. Simon trying to talk her into sleeping with him despite his marital status had killed any emotion she'd ever had for him.

He'd sneered at her wounded reaction to his intended infidelity. But having witnessed it up close with gut-wrenching frequency in her parents' marriage, she was well versed in its consequences.

Cutting Simon out of her life once she'd seen his true colours had been a painful but necessary decision.

Of course, without his business acumen she'd had to take full financial responsibility of Dolce Italia. Hence her search for Narciso Valentino. She needed him to stand by his company's promise. A contract was a contract....

A gleaming black limo was pulling up as she rounded the corner of the block that housed the nightclub. The journey had taken an extra half-hour because of a late-running train. Wincing at the pinch of her high heels on the uneven pavestones, she hurried towards Riga's red-bricked façade.

She was navigating her way around puddles left by the recent April shower, when deep male laughter snagged her attention.

A burly bouncer held open the velvet rope cordon as two men, both over six feet tall, exited the VIP entrance in the company of two strikingly beautiful women. The first man was arresting enough to warrant a second look but it was the other man who commanded Ruby's interest.

Jet-black hair had been styled to slant over the right side of his forehead in a silky wave that flowed back to curl over his collar.

Her steps faltered as the power of his presence slammed into her, and knocked air out of her lungs. His aura sent a challenge to the world, dared it to do its worst.

Dazed, she documented his profile—winged eyebrow, beautifully sculpted cheekbone, a straight patrician nose and a curved mouth that promised decadent pleasure—or what she imagined decadent pleasure looked like. But his mouth promised it and, well, this guy looked as if he could deliver on whatever sensual promises he made.

'Hey, miss. You coming in any time this century?'

The bouncer's voice distracted her, but not for long enough to completely pull her attention away. When she looked back, the man was turning away but it wasn't before Ruby caught another quick glimpse of his breathtaking profile.

Her gaze dropped lower. His dark grey shirt worn under a clearly bespoke jacket was open at the collar, allowing a glimpse of a bronzed throat and mouth-watering upper chest.

Ruby inhaled sharply and pulled her coat tighter around her as if that could stem the heat rushing like a breached dam through her.

The drop-dead gorgeous blonde smiled his way. His hand dropped from her waist to her bottom, drifted over one cheek to cup it in a bold squeeze before he helped her into the car. The first man shouted a query, and the group turned away from Ruby. Just like that, the strangely intimate and disturbing link was broken.

Her insides sagged and she realised how tight a grip she'd held on herself.

Even after the limo swung into traffic, Ruby couldn't move, nor could she stem the tingling suspicion that she'd arrived too late.

The bouncer cleared his throat conspicuously. She turned. 'Can you tell me who that second guy was who just got into that limo?' she asked.

He raised one *are-you-serious?* eyebrow.

Ruby shook her still-dazed head and smiled at the bouncer. 'Of course you can't tell me. Bouncer-billionaire confidentiality, right?'

His slow grin gentled his intimidating stature. 'Got it in one. Now, you coming in or you just jaywalking?'

'I'm coming in.' Although the strong suspicion that she'd missed Narciso Valentino grew by the second.

'Great. Here you go.' The bouncer placed a Mayan-mask-shaped stamp on her wrist, glanced up at her, then added another stamp. 'Show it at the bar. It'll get you your first drink on the house.' He winked.

She smiled in relief as she entered the smoky interior. If her guess had been wrong and she hadn't just missed Narciso Valentino, she could nurse an expensive drink while searching him out.

She'd worked in clubs like these all through college and knew how expensive even the cheapest drinks were. Which was why she clutched an almost warm virgin Tiffany Blue an hour later as she accepted that Narciso Valentino *was* the man she'd seen outside.

Resigned to her fruitless journey, she downed the last of her drink and was looking for a place to set the glass down when the voices caught her attention.

'Are you sure?'

'Of course I am. Narciso will be there.'

Ruby froze, then glanced into one of the many roped-off VIP areas. Two women dripping in expensive jewellery and designer dresses that would cost her a full year's salary sat sipping champagne.

Unease at her shameless eavesdropping almost forced her away but desperation held her in place.

'How do you know? He didn't attend the last two events.' The blonde looked decidedly pouty at that outcome.

'I told you, I overheard the guy he was with this evening talking about it. They're both going this time. If I can get a job as a *Petit Q* hostess, this could my chance,' her red-headed friend replied.

'What? To dress in a clown costume in the hope of catching his eye?'

'Stranger things have happened.'

'Well, hell will freeze over before I do that to hook a guy,' the blonde huffed.

Statuesque Redhead's lips pursed. 'Don't knock it till you try it. It pays extremely well. And if Narciso Valentino falls in my lap, well, let's just say I won't let that life-changing opportunity pass me by.'

'Okay, you have my attention. Give me the name of the website. And where the hell is Macau anyway?' the blonde asked.

'Umm…Europe, I think?'

Ruby barely suppressed a snort. Heart thumping, she took her phone from her tiny clutch and keyed in the website address.

An hour and a half later, she sent another Hail Mary and pressed send on the online forms she'd filled out on her return home.

It might come to nothing. She could fail whatever test or interview she had to pass to get this gig. Heck, after discovering that she was applying to hostess for *Q Virtus,* one of the world's most exclusive and secretive private clubs, she wondered if she didn't need her head examined. She could be wasting money and precious time chasing an elusive man. But she had to try. Each day she waited was another day her goal slipped from her fingers.

The alternative—bowing to the pressure from her mother to join the family business—was unthinkable. At best she would once again become the pawn her parents used to antagonise each other. At worst, they would try and drag her down into their celebrity-hungry lifestyle.

They'd made her childhood a living hell. And she only had to pass a billboard in New York City to see they were still making each other's lives just as miserable but taking pleasure in documenting the whole thing for the world to feast on.

The Ricardo & Paloma Trevelli Show was prime-time viewing. The fly-on-the-wall documentary had been running for as long as Ruby could remember.

When she was growing up, her daily routine had included

at least two sets of camera crews documenting her every move along with her parents'.

TV crews had become extended family members. For a very short time when it'd made her the most popular girl at school, she'd told herself she was okay with it.

Until her father's affairs began. His very public admission of infidelity when she was nine years old had made ratings soar. Her mother publicly admitting her heartbreak had made world-wide news. Almost overnight, the TV show had been syndicated worldwide and brought her parents even more notoriety.

The subsequent reunion and vow renewal had thrilled the world.

After her father's second admission of infidelity, millions of viewers had been given the opportunity to weigh in on the outcome of Ruby's life.

Strangers had accosted her on the street, alternatively pitying and shaming her for being a Trevelli.

Escaping to college at the opposite end of the country had been a blessing. But even then she hadn't been able to avoid her roots.

It'd quickly become apparent that she had no other talent than cooking.

The realisation that the Trevelli gene was truly stamped into her DNA was a deep fear she secretly harboured. It was the reason she'd cut Simon out of her life without a backward glance. It was also the reason she'd vowed never to let her parents influence her life.

Which was why she needed a ten-minute conversation with Narciso Valentino. A tingle of awareness shot through her as she replayed the scene outside Riga.

With a spiky foreboding, she recalled the dark, dangerously sensual waves vibrating off him; those bronzed, sure fingers drifting over the blonde's bottom, causing unwelcome heat to drag through Ruby's belly.

God, what was she doing lying in bed thinking of some stranger's hand on his girlfriend's ass?

She punched her pillow into shape and flipped off her bed-side lamp. She couldn't control the future but she could control the choice between mooning over elegant hands that looked as if they could bring a woman great pleasure or getting a good night's sleep.

She was almost asleep when her phone pinged an incoming message.

Exhaling in frustration, she grabbed the phone.

The brightness in the dark room hurt her eyes, but, even half blinded, Ruby could see the words clearly. Her CV had impressed the powers that be.

She'd been granted an interview to become a *Petit Q*.

CHAPTER TWO

Macau, China, One Week Later

THE RED FLOOR-LENGTH gown sat a little too snugly against Ruby's skin, and the off-the-shoulder design exposed more cleavage and general flesh than she was comfortable with. But after two gruelling interviews, one of which she'd almost blown by turning up late due to another delayed train, the last thing she could complain about was the expensive designer outfit that spelt her out as a *Petit Q*.

She was careful now to avoid it getting snagged on her heels as she walked across the marble floor of her hotel towards the meeting place, from where they'd be chauffeured to their final destination. In her small case were two carefully folded, equally expensive outfits the management had provided.

An examination had shown that they, too, like the dress she wore, would be tight...everywhere. It was clear that someone, somewhere in the management food chain had got her measurements very wrong.

She'd already attracted the attention of an aging rock star in the lift on the way to the ground floor of her Macau hotel. It didn't matter that he'd seemed half blind when he'd leered at her; attracting *any* attention at all made her stomach knot with acid anxiety.

She'd let her guard down with Simon, had believed his interest to be pure and genuine, only to discover he wanted nothing more than a bit on the side. The idea that he'd assumed because she was a Trevelli she would condone his indecent proposal, just as her mother continued to accept her father's, had shredded the self-esteem she'd fought so hard to attain when she'd removed herself from her parents' sphere.

She wasn't a coward, but the fear that she might never be able to judge another man's true character sent a cold shiver through her.

Pushing the thought away, she straightened her shoulders, but another troubling thought immediately took its place.

What if she'd made a huge mistake in coming here?

What if Narciso didn't show? What if he showed and she missed him again?

No, she had to find him. Especially in light of the phone call she'd received the morning after she'd signed on to be a *Petit Q*.

The voice had been calm but menacing. Simon had sold his twenty-five-per-cent share of her business to a third party. 'We will be in touch shortly about interest and payment terms,' the accented voice had warned.

'I won't be able to discuss any payment terms until the business is up and running,' she'd replied, her hands growing clammy as anxiety dredged her stomach.

'Then it is in your interest to make that happen sooner rather than later, Miss Trevelli.'

The line had gone dead before she could say anything more. For a moment, she'd believed she'd dreamt the whole thing, but she'd lived in New York long enough to know loan sharks were a real and credible threat. And Simon had sold his share in her business to one of them.

Panicked and angry with Simon, she'd been halfway across the Indian Ocean before she'd read her *Petit Q* guidelines and experienced a bolt of shock.

No doubt to protect its ultra-urban-legend status, the *Q Virtus* Macau caucus was to be a masked event at a secret location in Macau.

Masked, as in *incognito.* Where the chances of picking out Narciso Valentino would be hugely diminished.

The memory of broad shoulders and elegant fingers flashed across her mind. Yeah, sure, as if she were an expert in male shoulders enough to distinguish one from the other.

Her fingers clenched around her tiny red clutch. She'd come all this way. She refused to admit defeat.

The redhead from Riga turned towards her and Ruby fought not to grit her teeth as the other woman dismissed her instantly.

As the door to the Humvee limo slid shut behind them another jagged stab of warning pierced her. Every cell in her body screamed at her to abandon this line of pursuit and hightail it back home.

She could use the app to find out when Narciso returned to New York. She could confront him on home turf where she was more at ease, not here in this sultry, exotic part of the world where the very air held a touch of opulent magic.

But what if this was her last chance? A man who would fly thousands of miles for a highly secretive event could disappear just as easily given half a chance. She'd been lucky to be in the right place to find out where he'd be at this point in time.

Fate had handed her the opportunity. She wasn't going to blow it.

The limo hit a bump, bringing her back to reality.

Despite the glitzy lights and Vegas-style atmosphere, the tiny island of Macau held a charisma and steeped-in-history feel that had spilled over from mainland China. She held her breath as they crossed over the Lotus Bridge into Cotai, their final destination.

Bicycles raced alongside sports cars and nineteen-fifties buses in a spectacular blend of ancient and modern.

Less than ten minutes later, they rolled to a stop. Exiting, she looked around and her trepidation escalated. The underground car park was well lit enough to showcase top-of-the-line luxury sports cars and blinged-out four-by-fours next to stretch limos.

The net worth in the car park alone was enough to fund the annual gross domestic product of a small country.

The buzz of excitement in her group fractured her thoughts and she hurried forward into waiting lifts. Like her, the other nineteen hostesses were dressed in red gowns for the first evening, and the ten male hosts dressed in red jackets.

Six bodyguards accompanied them into the lifts and Ruby stemmed the urge to bolt as the doors started to close. Five seconds later it was too late.

The doors opened to gleaming parquet floors with red and gold welcoming carpet running through the middle of the vast, suspended foyer.

On the walls, exquisite tapestries of dragons flirting with maidens were embellished with multihued glass beads. Red and gold Chinese-silk cloth hung in swathes from the tapered ceiling to the floor, discreetly blacking out the outside world.

Two winged staircases led to the floor below where a sunken section in the middle had been divided into twelve gaming tables, each with its own private bar and seating area.

All around her, masked men in bespoke tuxedos mingled with exquisitely clad women dripping with stunning jewellery that complemented their breathtaking masks. Granted, the number of women was marginally less than men, but from the way they carried themselves Ruby suspected these women wielded more than enough power to hold their own against their male counterparts.

A tall, masked, jet-haired woman wearing a sophisticated-looking earpiece glided forward and introduced herself as Head Hostess. In succinct tones, she briefed them on their roles.

Ruby tried to calm her jangling nerves as she descended the stairs and headed for the bar of the fourth poker table.

A bar she could handle.

Nevertheless, she held her breath as the first group of men took their places at the table. They all wore masks in varying degrees of camouflage and design. As she mixed her first round of drinks and delivered it to the table, Ruby tried to glean if any of them resembled her quarry.

One by one, she dismissed them. Eventually, they drifted off and another group took their place.

A grey-haired man—the oldest in her group—immediately drew her attention. He carried himself with command and control, but he was too old to be Narciso Valentino and his frame was slightly stooped with age.

He snapped his fingers and threw out an order for a glass of Sicilian red. Ruby pursed her lips and admonished herself not to react to the rudeness. Five men took their places around the table, leaving only one other space to be filled.

Safely behind the bar after delivering their drinks order, she watched their bets grow larger and bolder.

Music pumped from discreet loud speakers, and through a set of double doors guests took to the dance floor. It wasn't deafening by any means but Ruby felt the pulse of the provocative music through the soles of her feet.

She swallowed down the mingled distaste and latent fear as she noticed things were beginning to get hot and heavy as guests began to loosen their inhibitions.

She could do this. Just because she was a Trevelli didn't mean she would lose sight of her goals. Decadence and excess were her parents' thing. They needn't be hers…

The lights overhead dimmed.

A door to one side of the lift labelled The Black Room swung open and two men stepped onto the gangway.

One wore a gold half-mask that covered him from forehead to nose. The aura of power that radiated from him raised the very temperature of the room.

But the moment Ruby's eyes encountered the second man, her belly clenched.

The head hostess drifted towards him but he raised a hand and waved her away. At the sight of those slim fingers, recognition slammed into her. She watched, dry-mouthed, as he sauntered down the steps and headed for her side of the room.

He stopped in front of her bar.

Silver eyes bore into hers, drilling down hard as if he wanted to know her every last secret. The smile slowly left his face as he continued to stare at her, one eyebrow gradually lifting in silent query.

His silver and black onyx mask was artistically and visually stunning. It revealed his forehead and the lower part of his face and against its brilliance his olive skin glowed in a way that made her want to touch that chiselled jaw.

Piercing eyes drifted over her in a lazy sweep, pausing for a long second at her breasts. Her breath hitched in her throat as her body reacted to his probing gaze.

Narciso Valentino. If she'd had two dollars to rub together she'd have bet on it.

Her mouth dried as she looked into his eyes and lost every last sensible thought in her head.

'Serve me, *cara mia*. I'm dying of thirst.' His voice was raw, unadulterated sin, oozing what Ruby could only conclude was sex appeal.

At least she thought so because the sound of it had transmitted a tingling to parts of her body she hadn't known could tingle just from hearing a man's voice. And why on earth had her hands grown so clammy?

When his brow arched higher at her inactivity, she scrambled to think straight. 'W-what would you like?'

His eyes moved down again, paused at her throat, where her pulse jumped like a frenzied rabbit.

'Surprise me.'

He turned abruptly and all signs of mirth leached from his face.

Across the small space between the bar and the poker table, he speared the silver-haired man with an unforgiving gaze.

The man stared back, the part of his face visible beneath his mask taut despite his whole body bristling with disdain.

Animosity arced through the air, snapping coils of dangerous electricity that made Ruby's pulse leap higher. Her gaze slid back to the younger man as if drawn by magnets. She told herself she was trying to decipher what sort of drink to make him but, encountering those broad shoulders again, her mind drifted into impure territory, as it had outside the nightclub in New York.

Focus!

The older man had requested a Sicilian red but instinctively she didn't think the man she'd concluded was Narciso would go for wine.

Casting her gaze over the bottles of spirits and liqueurs, she quickly measured the required shots, mixed a cocktail and placed it on a tray.

Willing her fingers not to shake, she approached the poker table and placed his drink at his elbow.

He dragged his gaze from the older man long enough to glance from the pale golden drink to her face. 'What is this?' he asked.

'It's a...*Macau Bombshell,*' she blurted out the name she'd come up with seconds ago.

One smooth brow spiked as he leaned back in his seat. 'Bombshell?' Once again, his gaze drifted over her, lingered at the place where her dress parted mid-thigh in a long slit. 'Would you place yourself in that category, too? Because you certainly have the potential.'

Right, so really he was one of those. A Playboy with a capital *P*.

A man who saw something he coveted and went for it, regardless of who got hurt. The clear image of his hand on another woman made her spine stiffen in negative reaction, even as a tiny part of her acknowledged her disappointment.

Irritated with herself, she pushed the feeling away.

Now she knew what sort of man she was dealing with, things would proceed much smoother.

'No, I wouldn't,' she said briskly. 'It's all about the drink.'

'I've never heard such a name.'

'It's my own creation.'

'Ah.' He sipped the champagne, falernum, lemon and pine-apple mix. Then he slowly tasted the cocktail without taking his eyes off her. 'I like it. Bring me one every half-hour on the button until I say otherwise.'

The implication that she could be here for hours caused her teeth to grind. She looked from the dealer to the other players at the table, wondered if she could ask to speak to Narciso privately now.

'Is there a problem?' he queried.

She cleared her throat. 'Well, yes. There are no clocks in this place and I don't have a watch, so…'

The silver-haired man swore under his breath and moved his shoulders in a blatantly aggressive move.

'Hold out your hand,' Narciso said.

Ruby's eyes widened. 'Excuse me?'

'Give me your hand,' he commanded.

She found herself obeying before she could think not to. He removed an extremely expensive and high-tech-looking watch from his wrist and placed it on her right wrist. The chain link was too large for her but it didn't mask the warmth from his skin and something jagged and electric sliced through her belly.

When his hand drifted along the inside of her wrist, she bit back a gasp, and snatched her hand back.

'Now you know when I'll next need you.'

'By all means, keep me waiting as you try out your tired pick-up lines,' the older man snapped with an accent she vaguely recognised.

Silver Eyes shifted his gaze to him. And although he continued to sip his cocktail, the air once again snapped with dark animosity.

'Ready for another lesson, old man?'

'If it involves teaching you to respect your betters, then I'm all for it.'

The resulting low laugh from the man next to her sent a shiver dancing over her skin. On decidedly wobbly legs, she retreated behind the bar and forced herself to regulate her breathing.

Whatever she'd experienced when those mesmerising eyes had locked into hers and those long fingers had stroked her was a false reaction. She refused to trust any emotion that could lead her astray.

Focus!

She glanced down at the watch. The timepiece was truly exquisite, a brand she'd heard of and knew was worth a fortune.

Unable to stop herself, she skated her fingers over it, her pulse thundering all over again when she remembered how he'd looked at her before slipping the watch on her wrist. She shifted as heat dragged through her and arrowed straight between her legs.

No!

She wasn't a slave to her emotions like her parents. And she wasn't the gullible fool Simon had accused her of being.

She had a goal and a purpose. One she intended to stick to.

Exactly half an hour later, she approached, willing her gaze not to trace those magnificent shoulders. Up close they were even broader, more imposing. When he shifted in his seat, they moved with a mesmerising fluidity that made her want to stop and gawp.

Keeping her gaze fixed on the red velvet table, she quickly deposited his drink on the designated coaster and picked up his almost-empty one. He flicked a glance at her.

'Grazie.'

The sound of her mother tongue on his lips flipped her stomach with unwanted excitement. She told herself it was because she was one step further to confirming his identity but Ruby suspected it was the sheer sexiness of his voice that was the bigger factor here.

'Prego,' she responded automatically before she could stop herself. She bit her lip and watched him follow the movement. A deeply predatory gleam entered his eyes.

'I want the next one in fifteen minutes.' His gaze returned

to his opponent, who looked a little paler since the last round of drinks. 'I have a feeling I'll be done by then. Unless you want to quit while you're behind?' he asked, sensual lips parted in a frightening imitation of a smile.

The older man let out a pithy response that Ruby didn't quite catch. Two players quickly folded their cards and left.

The two men eyeballed each other, pure hatred blazing as they psychologically circled one another.

Narciso laid down his cards in a slow, unhurried flourish. His opponent followed suit with a move that was eerily similar and made Ruby frown. The connection between the two men was unmistakable but she couldn't quite pin down why.

When the older man laughed, Ruby glanced down at his cards. She didn't know the rules of poker, but even she guessed his cards were significant.

She held her breath. Not with so much as a twitch did Narciso indicate he'd just lost millions of dollars.

'Give it up, old man.'

'*Mai!*' Never.

Ten minutes later, Narciso calmly laid down another set of cards that won him the next game. Hearing Giacomo's grunt of disbelief was extremely satisfactory. But it was the indrawn breath of surprise from the woman next to him that drew his attention.

He didn't let himself glance at her yet. She'd proven a seriously delicious distraction already. He had plans for her but those plans would have to wait a while longer.

For now, he revelled in Giacomo's defeat and watched a trickle of sweat drip down his temple.

They were barely an hour in and he'd already divested him of several million dollars. As usual, Giacomo had been lured in by the promise of trouncing his son, enabling Narciso to lay the bait he knew wouldn't be resisted.

The last game had won him a midsize radio station in Anaheim, California.

It would be a superb addition to his already sizeable news

and social media portfolio. Or he could shut it down and declare it a loss.

It didn't matter either way.

What mattered was that he had Giacomo's financial demise within his grasp. How very fitting that he should be in the perfect place to celebrate once he'd hammered the last nail into the coffin.

His gaze flickered to the stunning woman in red who regarded him with a touch of wariness and a whole lot of undisguised interest.

The silky cognac-coloured hair begged to be messed with, as did that sinful, pouting mouth she insisted on mauling every time he won a hand.

But her body, *Dio!* Her dress was a little too tight, sure, but even the fact that it made her assets a little too in your face didn't detract from the fact that she was a magnificent creature.

A magnificent creature he would possess tonight. She would be the cherry on his cake, one he would take the utmost pleasure in savouring before he devoured.

But first…

'Do you yield?' he asked silkily, already anticipating the response. In some ways they were so very similar. Which wasn't surprising considering they were father and son.

Although a father and son who detested the very ground each other walked on put an interesting twist on their *relationship*.

'Over my dead body.' Giacomo snapped his fingers at the dealer and threw his last five-million-dollar platinum chip in the middle of the table.

Beside him, his hostess's mouth dropped open. The sight of her pink tongue sent a spike of excitement through his groin.

Sì…he would celebrate well tonight. For a while there, he'd begun to suspect that beating Giacomo would be his only source of entertainment in Macau. Which was why he'd sought the old man out instead of leaving him to squirm a little longer. He'd wanted to be done and out of here as soon as possible.

The other deals he'd come to negotiate had taken the necessary leap forward and he'd believed there was nothing left.

But now…

His groin hardened as he watched her mouth slowly press shut and her eyes dart to his with the same anticipated excitement that flowed within him.

He let his interest show, let her see the promise of what was to come.

Heat flared up her delicate neck and flawless skin into a surprisingly innocent face that could've graced a priceless painting.

Dio, she was truly entrancing. And yet she was in a place like this, where the likelihood of being hit on, or more, was very real.

He gave a mental shrug. He'd stopped trying to reason why people took the actions they took well before he'd grown out of long socks.

Otherwise he'd have driven himself mad from trying to decipher why the father whose DNA flowed through his veins seemed to hate every single breath he took.

Or why Maria's betrayal still had the power to burn an acid path in his gut—

No.

That train had long left the station. Giving it thinking room was a waste of time and his time was extremely precious.

Keeping his eyes on his hostess, he downed his drink and held out his empty glass.

'I'm thirsty again, *amante.*'

With a nod, she sashayed away in her too-tight dress and returned minutes later with his drink.

When she started to move away, he snagged a hand around her waist. The touch of warm, silk-covered flesh beneath his fingers short-circuited his brain for a few moments. Then he realised she was trying to get away from him.

'Stay. You bring me luck when you're near.'

'Shame you need a woman to win,' Giacomo sneered.

Narciso ignored him and nodded to the dealer. He wanted this game to be over so he could pull this magical being tighter into his arms, feel her melt against him, his prize for emerging triumphant.

Giacomo threw his chip defiantly into the fray. Narciso's chest tightened with the anger that never quite went away. For as long as he remembered, his father had treated him like that chip—inconsequential, easily cast aside. Underneath all the anger and bitterness, a wound he'd thought healed cracked open.

Ignoring it, he calmly plucked his cards from the table.

'Let's up the stakes.'

Eyes that had once been similar to his own but had grown dimmer with age snapped at him. 'You think you have something I want?'

'I *know* I do. That tech company you lost to me last month? If I lose this hand, I'll return it to you, along with all of this.' He nodded to the pile of chips in front of him, easily totalling over thirty million dollars.

'And if I lose?' His voice held a false confidence Narciso almost smiled at. *Almost.*

'You hand over the other five-million chip I know is in your pocket and I'll let you keep your latest Silicon Valley start up.'

Giacomo sneered but Narciso could see him weighing up the odds. Thirty million against ten.

He waited, let the seductive scent of his hostess's perfume wash over him. Unable to resist, he slid his hand lower. The faintest sensation of a thong made his groin tighten. Again, she tried to move away. He pulled her back towards him and heard her breath catch.

'My offer expires in ten seconds,' he pressed.

Giacomo reached into his tuxedo pocket and tossed the second chip onto the table. Then he laid out cards in a flourish.

Four of a kind.

Narciso didn't need to glance down at his own cards to know *he'd* won.

And yet...the triumph he should've experienced was oddly missing. Instead, hollowness throbbed dully in his chest.

'Come on, then, you coward. It's your turn to answer this—do you yield?'

Narciso breathed in deep and fought the tight vice crushing his chest. Slowly, the hollowness receded and anger rushed into its place. 'Yes, I yield.'

His father's bark of victorious laughter drew attention from other tables but Narciso didn't care.

His hand was tightening over her waist, anticipation of a different sort firing his body. He was about to turn towards her when Giacomo reached for the cards Narciso had discarded.

A straight flush. A winning hand more powerful than his father's.

The evidence that he'd been toyed with registered in Giacomo's shocked eyes. *'Il diavolo!'* He lunged across the table, his whole body vibrating with fury.

Narciso stood, his eyes devoid of expression. *'Sì,* I am the devil *you* spawned. You'll do well to remember that next time we meet.'

CHAPTER THREE

I AM THE devil you *spawned.*

Had he meant that literally?

Ruby glanced at the man who had her imprisoned against his side as he steered her towards…

'Where are you taking me?' she demanded in a rush as electrifying fingers pressed more firmly into her skin. Who knew silk was an excellent conductor of heat?

She burned from head to toe and he wasn't even touching her bare skin.

'First to the dance floor. And then…who knows?'

'But my duties…behind the bar—'

'Are over,' he stated imperiously.

Despite the alien emotions swirling through her, she frowned. 'Can you do that?'

'You'll find that I can pretty much do anything I want.'

'You deliberately lost thirty million dollars two minutes ago. I think doing what you want is pretty obvious. What I'm asking is, am I risking my job by deserting my post?'

He ushered her into the lift, took hold of her wrist and held the smartwatch against the panel. When it lit up, he pressed the key for the floor below. 'You're here to serve the members of this club. I require your services on the dance floor. There, does that ease your anxiety?' He asked the question with a thread of cynicism that made her glance closely at him.

The tic throbbing at his temple and tense shoulders indicated that he hadn't shrugged off his encounter at the poker table.

'Who was that man you were playing with?' she asked.

Silver eyes hardened a touch before they cleared and he smiled. Ruby forced herself not to gulp at the pulse-destroying transformation his smile achieved.

'No one important. But you—' he faced her fully as the lift stopped and the doors glided open '—are much more fascinating.'

One hand brushed her wrist and slid up her arm. The shiver when he'd first touched her returned a hundredfold, sending soul-deep tremors through her.

What on earth was going on? She'd believed herself in love with Simon, enough to come within a whisper of making a fool of herself, and yet he'd not triggered an iota of what she was feeling now.

Chemistry.

The word fired alarm bells so loud in her head she jerked backwards. Her back hit the lift wall and panic flared high as he stepped closer. Heat waves bounced off his hard-packed, unapologetically male body straight into hers.

'I'm not fascinating. Not in the least,' she said hurriedly.

He laughed, a deep, husky sound that sent warning tingling all over her body.

Was this how helpless prey felt within the clutches of a merciless predator? She was nobody's prey; nonetheless she couldn't deny this man's seriously overwhelming presence.

'You're refreshingly naïve, too.' His gaze probed, then his smile slowly faded. Although the hunger didn't. 'Unless *that's* the ploy?' he queried in the same silky tone he'd used at the poker table.

Ruby's breath caught as the unmistakable sense of danger washed over her again. 'There's no ploy. And I'm not naïve.'

His fingers had reached her shoulder. They skated along her collarbone, perilously close to the pulse jumping at her throat.

The doors started to slide shut. His fingers stopped just shy of touching her pulse, then returned to grasp her wrist. With a tap on the smartwatch the doors parted again.

'Come and dance with me. You can tell me how un-naïve and un-fascinating you are.'

He led her to the middle of a dance floor much larger than the one upstairs. Over a dozen guests graced the large space, moving to the beat of the sultry blend of Far Eastern music and western jazz.

They could've danced apart. In fact Ruby was counting on the brief reprieve from close contact. But he had other ideas.

He caught her close, one arm around her waist and the other catching her hand and imprisoning it against his chest as he began to sway. The fluidity with which he moved, his innate sensuality, told her that this man knew a lot about sex and sexuality. Would know how to take a woman and leave her utterly replete but desperate for more.

'I'm waiting for you to enlighten me.'

For a second she couldn't get her brain to work. Sensations she'd never felt before crashed through her as his hard thighs brushed hers.

'About what?'

'About why you think you're not fascinating. Those impure thoughts running through your head we'll leave for later.'

She sucked in a shocked breath. 'How…? I wasn't…'

'You blush when you're flustered. As endearing as that is, you'd make a lousy poker player.'

'I don't gamble. And I don't know why I'm having this conversation with you.'

'We're performing the requisite mating dance before we… mate.'

She stopped dead. 'In your dreams! I'm not here to be your, or anyone's, appetiser.'

'Don't sell yourself short, sweetheart. I'd place you more as a deliciously forbidden dessert than an appetiser. But one I intend to devour nonetheless.'

She was on a dance floor thousands of miles away from home, immersed in a debate about which food course she was.

Surreal didn't even begin to cover the emotions coursing through her as she glanced up at him and encountered that blatantly masculine square jaw and those hypnotic eyes.

'Look, Mr...?'

He raised a brow. 'You're at a masked event, shrouded in secrecy, embroiled in intrigue and mystery, and you want to know my name?' he asked cynically.

Damn, how could she have forgotten? 'Why do I get the feeling that all this bores you rigid?'

His eyes gleamed. 'How very intuitive of you. You're right—it does Or it did, until I saw you.'

Her heart gave a little kick. One she determinedly ignored. 'You were fully engaged when you played your game. And *that* had nothing to do with me.'

Again that reminder hardened his eyes. 'Ah, but I lost thirty million dollars so I could make what's happening between us happen sooner.'

'There's nothing happening—'

'If you believe *that* then you really are naïve.'

Another couple danced closer. The flash of red hair distracted Ruby enough to make her look. *Redhead* was in the arms of another man but her hungry eyes were fixed squarely on Narciso.

Irrational irritation jerked up Ruby's spine.

Pursing her lips, she tilted her chin at the redhead. 'Why don't you help yourself to her? She definitely wants you.'

He didn't bother to glance where Ruby indicated. He merely smiled and shrugged. 'Every woman wants me.'

'Wow, you're not the shy type at all, are you?' she snapped.

He leaned forward, and a swathe of luxurious black hair fell over his forehead to curl over the top of his mask. 'Are those the types that turn you on?' he whispered.

The image of shy, self-effacing...*duplicitous* Simon fleeted across her mind. She stiffened. 'We're not discussing my tastes here.'

'I've clearly hit a nerve. But if you don't tell me what your tastes are, how will I know how to please you?' His mouth was a hair's breadth from her ear.

Ruby fought to breathe. Her chest was a mere inch from his but her lower body was plastered against his in a way that made his body's response blatant and unmistakable.

He was aroused. And he meant her to know it.

Her abdomen clenched so forcefully, she lost her footing and stumbled.

Strong hands righted her and began to pull her back into his arms but Ruby quickly stepped back.

'You can start by buying me a drink.'

He reluctantly dropped his hand from her waist. Expecting overwhelming relief, Ruby frowned when it didn't arrive.

A white-jacketed waiter hovered nearby. 'Champagne?'

She shook her head. 'No. Something else.'

Something that would take several minutes to make and give her time to get her perplexing emotions under control.

'State what you wish,' he said.

She almost blurted her reason for being in Macau there and then. But this wasn't the right time. She needed to get him alone, in a place where he couldn't blow her off as easily as his employees had these past weeks.

Casting her gaze around, she pointed to the far side of the room. 'There.'

'The ice-vodka lounge? Is this a delaying tactic?'

'Of course not. I really want a drink.'

He watched her for several seconds, then he nodded.

This time her relief was tangible. But the reprieve didn't last long. His arm slid possessively around her waist as he led her off the dance floor.

She was suppressing the rising tide of that damned *chemistry* when he leaned in close. 'You're only trying to delay the inevitable, *tesoro*.'

'I have no idea what you mean.'

His laughter drew gazes and turned heads. Ruby had a feeling everything this man did compelled attention. And not just of the female variety.

Powerful men stepped aside as he steered her towards the vodka lounge. A faux-fur coat appeared as if by magic and he draped it over her shoulders before they entered the sub-zero room. She headed for an empty slot at the bar, near an ice sculpture carved in the shape of a Chinese dragon.

The bartender glanced at her unmasked face with a frown.

'I'd like a *Big Apple Avalanche*, please. Heavy on the apple.' She needed a clear head if she intended to stay toe to toe with Narciso Valentino.

The bartender didn't move. 'I don't think you're allowed—'

'Is there a problem?' The hard rasp came from over her shoulder.

The bartender snapped to attention. 'Not at all, sir.' He grabbed the apple mixer and the canister of top-range vodka.

'I'll take it from here.' Narciso took the drinks from him and waved him away.

Despite the warmth of her coat, she shivered when he turned to her.

'Ready?'

God, this wasn't going well at all. Far from feeling under control, she felt her thoughts scatter to the wind every time he looked into her eyes.

'Yes,' she said as she inserted the specialised drinking spout into the ice outlet and brought her lips to it.

Her eyes met molten silver ones and fiery heat rushed into her belly. He slowly tipped the canister and icy vodka and apple pooled into her mouth.

Cold and heat simultaneously soothed and burned their way down her throat but the power of the decadent drink came nowhere close to the potent gleam in his eyes.

Before discovering Simon's duplicity, sex had been something she'd imagined in abstract terms; something she'd accepted would eventually happen between them, once the trust and affection she'd thought was growing between them was solid enough to lean on.

Sex just for the sake of it, or used as a weapon the way she'd watched her parents use it, had made being a virgin at twenty-four an easy choice.

But looking into Narciso's eyes, she slowly began to understand why sex was a big deal for some women. Why they dwelled on it with such single-minded ferocity.

Never had she wanted to drown in a man's eyes. Never had she wanted to kiss sensually masculine lips the way she wanted to kiss him right now. She wanted to feel those arms around her again, holding her prisoner the way they'd held her on the dance floor. She wanted to spear her fingers through his luxurious hair, scrape her nails over his scalp and find out if it brought him pleasure.

'Have another one,' he commanded huskily. He raised the sterling silver mixer, his gaze riveted on her mouth.

He wanted to kiss her badly. The same way she wanted to kiss him. Or would have if she didn't know from painful experience how treacherous and volatile sexual attraction could be.

'No, thanks. It's getting late. I need to go.'

One beautifully winged brow rose. 'You need to go.'

'Yes.'

'And where *exactly* do you intend to go?'

She frowned. 'Back to my hotel, of course.'

He slowly lowered his arm. 'I thought you understood your role here,' he murmured coolly.

Icy foreboding shivered down her spine. 'What's that supposed to mean?'

'It means, the moment the last guest arrived, the whole building went into lock down. You're stuck here with me until tomorrow at six.' He discarded the canister and stepped closer. 'And I have the perfect idea of how we can pass the time.'

* * *

Narciso watched a myriad expressions dart over her face.

Excitement. Anxiety. Suspicion.

Two of those three weren't what he expected from a woman when he announced they were effectively locked in together. Most women would be salivating at the thought and making themselves available before he changed his mind.

Not this one.

Even the hint of excitement was fading. Now she just looked downright frightened.

He frowned. 'I expected a more enthusiastic response.'

Her gaze went to the watch—his watch—then back to his face. Narciso decided not to think about why the sight of his large watch on her delicate wrist pleased him so much.

He would gift it to her. She could keep it on during sex. Once he'd dispelled that unacceptable look from her face.

'You just told me I can't leave. And you expect me to be excited?'

'You have some of the world's richest and most influential men gathered in one place. Everyone who attends these events has the same agenda—network hard and party harder, especially the *Petit Qs*. You, on the other hand, are acting as if you've received a prison sentence. Why?'

Her eyelids lowered and she grabbed the lapels of her coat.

Faint alarm bells rang at the back of his mind. Going against a habit of a lifetime, he forced himself to ignore it as she raised those delicate lids to lock gazes with him.

Her sapphire-blue eyes held a combination of boldness and shyness that hugely intrigued him. She wanted something but wasn't quite sure how to get it.

He had every intention of showing her how to get exactly what she wanted once he got her to his suite upstairs. He might even tempt her into using the velvet ropes that held back his emperor-size bed's drapes...

Desire slammed into him with a force he hadn't experienced

in years…if ever. The strength of it struck him dumb for a few seconds before he realised she was speaking.

'…knew about the club, of course, and that my hostessing gig was for two days. I didn't know I'd be staying here for the duration.'

'Ah, one small piece of advice. Always read the small print.'

Her delicious mouth pursed. He had the sudden, clamouring urge to find out if it tasted as succulent as it looked. Her narrowed-eyed glare stopped him. Barely.

'I always do. I can't say the same for other people though. Especially people who have the small print pointed out to them and still wilfully ignore it.'

The alarm bells grew louder. 'That's decidedly…pointed. Care to elaborate?'

She opened her mouth, then shut it again. 'I'm cold. Can we leave?'

'That's an excellent idea.' He walked her to the door of the ice bar and helped her out of her coat.

The sight of her hardened nipples—an effect of the sub-zero temperature—fried a few million brain cells. That clawing hunger gutted him further, making him fight to remember whether he was coming or going.

Going. Definitely. Up to his allocated suite with this woman who sparked a reaction within him that left him reeling, and wanting more. He hadn't wanted anything this badly for a long time. Not since his eleventh birthday…

He shut off his thoughts and walked her to the lift, absurdly pleased when she didn't protest. Perhaps she'd accepted the inevitable.

They were meant to be together. Here in this place where the events of earlier this evening with Giacomo had nearly soured his experience.

She would take away the bitterness for a while. Take away his unsettling hollowness when he'd held the old man's financial demise in his grasp but hadn't taken it.

All would be better in the morning.

For tonight, he intended to seek the most delicious oblivion.

'Should I bother to ask where you're taking me now?'

His smile felt tight and his body on edge. 'No. Don't bother. What you should ask is how many ways will I make you like what's coming next.' He activated the electronic panel. When the chrome panel slid back to reveal the row of buttons he selected the fiftieth floor for his penthouse suite.

'If you're planning to throw a few more millions away, then I'd rather not watch.' Again there was that censorious note in her voice that strummed his instincts.

From experience he knew women always had hidden agendas, be it the urge to make themselves indispensable in his life the moment he so much as smiled their way or to take advantage of his power and influence—as well as his body—for as long as possible.

But the woman in front of him was exhibiting none of those traits. And yet there was something... Narciso didn't like the mixed signals he was receiving from her.

'Have we met before?' he demanded abruptly, although he was sure he would have remembered. She had an unforgettable body, and that mouth... He was absolutely certain he would have remembered that mouth.

'Met? No, of course not. Besides, I don't know who you are, remember?'

'If you don't know who I am then how do you know we haven't met before?'

Her eyes shifted away from his. 'I...don't know. I just think a man like you...I'd have remembered...that's all.'

He smiled at her flustered response, deciding he definitely liked her flustered. 'I like that you think I'm unforgettable. I aim to make that thought a permanent reality for you.'

'Trust me, you already have,' she quipped.

Narciso got the distinct impression it wasn't a compliment.

He stepped forward. She stepped back. Her eyes widened when she realised she was trapped against the wall of the lift.

His pulse thundered when her gaze darted to his mouth and then back to his eyes.

'Somewhere along the line, I seem to have made a bad impression on you. Normally I wouldn't care but...' He stepped closer, until the warmth of her agitated exhalations rushed over his chin. Her scent hit his nostrils and he nearly moaned at the seductive allure of it.

'But...?' she demanded huskily.

'But I find myself wanting to alter that impression.'

'You want me to think you're a good guy?'

Laughing, he slid his hand around her trim waist. 'No. *Good* is taking things a touch too far, *amante*. I haven't been *good* since...' he blunted that knife of memory again '...for ever.'

Her darkened eyes dropped to his mouth again and Narciso barely stopped himself from groaning. But he couldn't stop his hands from tightening on her waist. In contrast to her lush hips, her waist was so tiny, his hands spanned it easily.

'Then what do you want from me?'

Before he could succinctly elaborate, the lift doors slid open. The double doors leading into his suite beckoned. Beyond that the bedroom where he intended to make her his.

He grasped her wrist and tugged her after him. Using the smartwatch to activate the smaller panel, he pressed his thumb against the infrared scanner and pushed the doors open. He didn't bother to shut it because the doors were automatic. Security was exemplary at all *Q Virtus* events, especially the private suites. He had the whole floor to himself and no one would disturb them unless he wanted them to.

And he had no desire for any interruptions—

He noticed she'd stopped dead and turned to find her staring at him.

'You've brought me to your suite,' she blurted.

The pulse pounding at her throat could've been excitement. Or more likely it was the trepidation he'd seen earlier.

'Very observant of you.'

'Know this now—I won't be indulging in anything…illicit with you.'

'Since we haven't established exactly what it is we'll be doing I think we're getting a little ahead of ourselves.'

'I wish you'd stop toying with me.'

His shoulders moved with the restlessness that vibrated through his whole being. He couldn't remember the last time he'd had to work this hard to get a woman to acknowledge her interest in him. 'Fine. Do you deny that there's something powerful and undeniable happening between us?'

'I don't want—'

'If you really don't want to be here, say the word and I'll let you leave.' That wasn't strictly true. First he'd use his infinite skills to convince her to stay. Arrogance didn't come into his awareness that he was attractive to most women, and, despite her mixed signals, this woman was as attracted to him as he was to her.

She might need a little more work than usual—and the thought wasn't unpleasing—but he was more than up to the task.

He watched her debate with herself for an endless minute. Then she turned towards the window.

Narciso forced himself to remain still, despite his every cell screeching at him to grab her. Picking up a control device, he pushed the button that allowed the glass windows to turn from opaque to transparent.

Macau City lay spread before them in a cascade of lights, glittering water and awe-inspiring ancient Portuguese, Chinese and modern architecture.

Since he'd started doing business here, his fascination with the city had grown along with his bank balance.

But right now his fascination with her was much more paramount.

'Tell me you'll stay.' His voice emerged rougher than normal.

The thought that he wanted her badly, alarm bells or no alarm bells, made him frown. He'd trained himself not to want anything he absolutely could not have. It was why he calculated his every decision with scalpel-like precision.

That way he avoided disappointment. Avoided…heartache…

She turned from the window, arms crossed at that tiny waist. Her response took a minute, two at a stretch, but they were the longest minutes of Narciso's life.

'I'll stay…for a little while.'

He swallowed and nodded. Suddenly, his fingers itched to remove the pins in her hair, to see its silky dark gold abundance cascade over her shoulders.

'Take your hair down,' he instructed. The time for playing was over.

Her eyes widened. 'Why?'

'Because I want to see it. And because you're staying.'

Her fingers touched the knot at the back of her head. Anticipation spiked through him only to be doused in disappointment when she lowered her hand.

'I prefer to keep it up.'

'If you're trying to keep me hyped up with interest, trust me, it's working.'

'I'm not, I mean… My hair is no big deal.'

'It is to me. I have a weakness for long hair.'

Her head tilted to one side, exposing a creamy neck he longed to explore. 'If I take my hair down, will you take your mask off?'

As much as he wanted to rip his mask off, something told him to delay the urge. 'No,' he replied. 'My house, my rules.'

'That's not fair, is it?'

'If life was fair you'd be naked and underneath me by now.'

A blush splashed up her exquisite throat and stung her cheeks. Molten lust rushed into his groin and spread through his body. Feeling restricted and seriously on edge, he shrugged off his tuxedo jacket and flung it over the long sofa. Next came the bow tie. He left that dangling to tackle the top buttons of his shirt and looked up to find her gaze riveted on him.

Good, he was not alone in this. Sexual desire pulsed from

her in drenching waves. Which made the reticence in her eyes all the more intriguing.

Enough!

In three strides, he stood in front of her. She made a high, surprised noise as he tugged her close. Without giving her a chance to protest further, he swooped down and took her lips with his.

She tasted glorious. Like a shot of premium tequila on a sultry night. Like warm sunshine and decadent, sticky desserts. Like jumping off the highest peak of an icy mountain with nothing beneath him but air and infinite possibilities.

Narciso's lids slid shut against the drugging sensation of her lips.

Madre di Dio! He was hard. Harder than he'd ever been. And he'd only been kissing her a few seconds.

She made another sound in her throat and her lips parted. Her tongue darted out to meet his and he plunged in, desperate for more, desperate to discover her every secret.

He deepened the kiss and groaned as her hands slid up his biceps to entwine around his shoulders. In a curiously innocent move, she tentatively caressed his nape before boldly spiking her fingers into his hair.

The scrape of her fingers against his scalp made him shudder with escalating arousal. Raising his head, he gazed down into eyes darkened with desire. *'Amante,* you already know what pleases me.'

Shock clouded her expression, as if what she'd achieved had stunned her.

Without giving her a chance to speak, he took her luscious mouth again. The highly potent sound of their kisses echoed in the room as they devoured each other.

Pulling her even closer, he finally touched the pulse that had taunted him all evening. It sang beneath his touch, racing with her excitement.

She inhaled deeply, and her breasts smashed against his

chest. He cupped one, glorying in the weight and perfect fit of it as his thumb brushed across one rigid nub.

She jerked and her teeth sank into her bottom lip. With a rough sound, she pulled away.

Narciso continued to play with her nipple as they stared at each other. Her mouth, wet and slightly swollen, parted as she sucked in panicked breaths.

'You like the way I make you feel?' He brought his other hand up from her waist and cupped her other breast, attending to the equally stiff and aching peak. 'I promise I will make you feel even better. Now take your hair down and show me how gorgeous you really are.'

The words pulled Ruby from the drugged stupor she was drowning in. Reality didn't rush in, it trickled in slowly.

Blinking eyelids heavy with desire, she tried to focus on something other than his arrestingly gorgeous face—the part not covered by his mask.

First, she noticed the stunning chandelier. Then a repeat of that bold dragon motif from downstairs on the wall behind his shoulder. Reality rushed in faster. Stunningly designed black velvet sofas, including an authentic French chaise longue perfect for reclining in...

Then her focus drew in closer. She glanced down at the powerful hands cupping her breasts.

The sight was so erotically intoxicating it nearly knocked her off her feet.

Sensation shot between her thighs, stinging so painfully, she wanted to place her hand there, seek some sort of relief.

'Take your hair down for me,' he insisted again.

She came plunging back down to earth. 'No!'

Telling herself she didn't care about the jaw that tightened in displeasure, she took several steps away from his hot, tempting body.

Focus, Ruby!

The last time she'd mixed business with pleasure, she'd almost ended up becoming the one thing she despised above all else—a participant in infidelity. It didn't matter that she hadn't known Simon was married. The very thought of what could've happened made shame lodge in her belly.

She was here to get Narciso Valentino to honour his deal with her, not to get pulled into the same dangerous vortex of emotions that led to nothing but pain and heartache.

Her father's inability to limit his sexual urges to his marital bed and her mother's indecision whether to fight or turn a blind eye had made her childhood a living hell. It'd been the reason why she'd slept most nights with her headphones on and music blaring in her ears. Even then she'd been unable to block out the blistering rows or her mother's heart-wrenching sobs.

And after her experience with Simon, there was no way would she allow herself to jump on that unpredictable roller coaster.

She took another step back, despite the magnetic pull of desire dragging her to Narciso. Despite the soul-deep notion that sex with him would be pulse-poundingly breathtaking. Despite—

Despite nothing!

Her treacherous genetic make-up didn't mean she would allow herself to fall into the same trap as her mother just because an unrepentant, unscrupulous playboy like Narciso Valentino crooked his wicked finger.

But she couldn't risk alienating him before she got what she'd come here for. Licking tingling lips, she forced her brain to track.

She cast her gaze around the large, luxuriously appointed suite. Seeing the extensive, well-stocked bar on the far side of the room, she made a beeline for it. 'Here, let me get you another drink.'

'You don't need to get me drunk to have your way with me, *amante.*'

She flushed and stopped, whirling to find him directly behind her. The sheer size of him, the arousal stamped so clearly in his eyes, made her breath fracture. 'Stop calling me that.'

A small smile played around his exquisite mouth. 'You know what it means.'

She nodded. 'Yes, I'm Italian.'

'And I'm Sicilian. Big difference, but we will speak your language for now.'

'Whatever language we speak, I don't want you referring to me as a…as your…'

'Lover?'

'Yes. I don't like it.'

'What do you want me to call you?'

'Just call me Ruby.' She didn't mind telling him her name. In order to explain her presence here, she would have to disclose who she was.

So no harm done.

'Ruby.'

Definitely lots and lots of harm done. The way he said her name—wrapped his mouth and tongue around it in a slow caress—made her pulse leap crazily.

'Ruby. It suits you perfectly,' he murmured.

Against her will, his response drew her interest. 'How do you mean?'

'Your name matches the shade of your mouth after I've thoroughly kissed it. I imagine the same would apply to other parts of your body by the time we're done.'

Her flush deepened. *'Seriously?'*

He laughed but the hunger in his eyes didn't abate. 'Too much?'

'*Much* too much.'

He shrugged and nodded to the bar. 'I'll give you the reprieve you seek. But only for a little while.'

She dived behind the bar and gathered the first bottles that came to hand. Almost on automatic she replicated one of her favourite creations and slid it across the shiny surface.

He picked it up and sipped without taking his eyes off her.

He rolled the drink in his mouth before his eyes slowly widened. 'You're very talented.'

Pleasure rushed through her. 'Thank you.'

'Prego.' He threw back the rest of the drink and set the glass down with a decisive click. 'But enough with the foreplay, Ruby. Come here.'

Heart pounding, with nowhere to hide, she approached him.

'Give me what I want. Now.'

She debated for a tense few seconds. Then, figuring she had nothing to lose, she complied.

Her hair was thick, long and often times unmanageable. She'd spent almost an hour wrestling it into place tonight and in the end had chosen to wear it up. Her effort to straighten it would've worn out by now, and she couldn't help but fidget when his gaze raked over the golden-brown tresses once, twice and over again.

'You're exquisite,' he breathed after an endless moment during which her stomach churned with alien emotion. 'Your skin is flawless and I want to drown in your eyes, watch them light up with pleasure when I take you.'

Ruby couldn't believe mere words could create such heat inside her. Hell, everything about him made her hot and edgy.

She needed to nip this insanity in the bud before it went any further. 'I'm sorry if I gave you the impression that something more was going to happen between us. You won't be... taking me.'

'Will I not?' he asked silkily, his finger drifting down her cheek to settle beneath her chin. 'And what makes you say that?'

'Because you don't really want me.'

His laugh was rich, deep and incredibly seductive.

'Every nerve in my body disagrees with that statement. But if you need proof...' He bent low, scooped her up and threw her over his shoulder.

His laughter increased at her outraged squeal. 'Put me down!'

The hallway passed in a blur as he took her deeper into the

suite. Her hair entangled with his long legs as he strode with unwavering purpose.

'I don't know what the hell you think you're doing but I demand you put me down right—' Her breath whooshed out of her lungs as she was dumped on a bed. A very large emperor-size bed with slate-coloured sheets and over a dozen pillows.

'You were saying?'

She brushed her hair out of her eyes and saw him tugging off his shoes. When he unhooked his belt, she scrambled off the bed.

He caught her easily and placed her back in the centre. 'Are you going to be a good girl and wait for me?' Silver eyes speared her.

'Wait for… Hell, no!'

He stepped forward and caught her chin in his hand. When his head started to descend, she jerked away. 'What the hell do you think you're doing?'

'Capturing your attention for a moment. You don't need to be frightened, *dolce mia*. Nothing will happen in this room without your consent.'

Oddly, she believed him. 'You don't need to kiss me to capture my attention.'

Slowly he straightened and dropped his hand. 'Shame. Let me remind you of some ground rules before we proceed. We're not supposed to reveal ourselves to each other. However, since you've done me the honour of revealing your name to me, I'll grant you the courtesy of removing my mask. But you'll give me your word that it will stay between us, *si?*' He started unbuttoning his shirt, revealing mouth-watering inches of golden skin.

Heat slammed into her chest and she sucked in a gulping breath.

Crunch time. Time to get this dangerously bizarre situation over and done with.

'There's no need. I already know who you are. You're Narciso Valentino. You're the reason I'm here in Macau.'

CHAPTER FOUR

HE FROZE AT her announcement. A second later, he drew the mask over his head, and Ruby got her first full glimpse of Narciso Valentino.

He was breathtakingly gorgeous. With a definite edge of danger that sent her already thundering pulse straight into bungee-jump mode.

She watched his face grow taut. Watchful…condemning.

'You know who I am.' His words were icily precise, the warmth in his tone completely gone.

Licking dry lips, she nodded. His other hand dropped from his belt, leaving her curiously disappointed.

'You're American.'

'Yes, I live in New York, same as you. That's where I came from.'

'And you followed me all the way to Macau. Why?' The clipped demand came with eyes narrowed into cold slits.

A mixture of anger and trepidation rushed through her, propelling her from the bed.

He caught her easily. 'Move again and I'll be forced to restrain you.'

Panic flared through her. Tugging at his hands, she fought to free herself. Before she could fathom his intentions, her wrists were bound to the bedpost with velvet rope he'd pulled from the side of the bed.

She looked from her wrists to his face, unable to believe what was happening. He tossed his mask on the bed, whipped the unbound tie from his neck and flung it across the room, barely suppressed fury in the movement. 'Okay, fine, you've made your point. But you can't keep me prisoner for ever.'

'Watch me.'

'I could scream, you know.'

Nice, Ruby. Nice.

'You could. And I can turn you over to the management and let them deal with what can only be regarded as a security breach. Trust me, breaches aren't taken lightly.'

She tugged at her bound wrists. 'I can't believe you tied me up.'

'You left me no choice. Now start talking before I call security.'

Her breath caught as images tumbled through her head of being stuck in a foreign prison. Aside from her roommate, Annie, no one knew her whereabouts. And even if Annie tracked her down to Macau, she wouldn't have the first clue where to find her.

'Tell me what you want to know,' she offered in a rush.

'Is Ruby really your name?' he asked, his gaze dropping to her lips.

Remembering what he'd said about her mouth, she felt heat spike through her belly again.

'Yes.'

'And your earlier assurance that we hadn't met before?'

'Is true. Although we almost did…last week.'

One sleek brow shot upward. 'How?'

'I tried to find you at a nightclub—Riga—but you were leaving when I arrived.'

He prowled closer to the bed, and a fresh load of anxiety coursed through her system. Hands poised on lean hips, he stared down at her.

'I've had women do…unexpected things to get my attention but I don't think I've had the privilege of a full-blown crazy stalker before.' His eyes raked her from head to toe. 'Perhaps I should've made it happen sooner.'

'I'm not a crazy stalker!' She yanked at the restraints and only succeeded in tightening them.

'Of course not. Because those ones readily admit to their charges.'

'Look, I can explain. Just…untie me.'

He ignored her and leaned down, placing his palms flat on the bed so his face was level with hers. 'We could've had so much fun, *amante*. Why did you have to spoil it?' There was genuine regret in his tone, but bitterness had crept in with the iciness.

'I have a genuine reason for being here.'

'For your own sake, I hope so. I don't take lightly to being manipulated.'

Her mind flashed to earlier in the evening. Watching him toy with his opponent had shown her just how dangerous this man was. Despite the outward charm and spellbinding magnetism, he could become lethal on the turn of a dime.

He turned and prowled to the window. With jerky movements, he tore off his expensive shirt, sending cufflinks she was almost certain were made with black diamonds pinging across the room.

Tossing the shirt the way his bow tie had gone, he shoved his hands into his pockets.

The movement contracted his bronzed, strongly muscled back. Among the electrons firing crazily in her brain came the thought that this was the first time she'd come this close to a semi-naked man worth looking at.

He turned and the sight of his naked torso was almost too much to bear. A light smattering of hair grew outward from the middle of his sculpted chest and arrowed down to disappear into his waistband.

Heat intensified as her gaze landed on his flat brown nipples. A decadent shudder coursed through her. She grasped the sturdy, intricately carved bedpost made of highly polished Chinese cedarwood, pulled herself closer to the edge of the bed and peered closer at the intricate knots that bound her.

'Where do you think you're going?' he rasped.

'I can't stay trussed up like a Thanksgiving turkey all night long.'

'Answer my questions and I'll consider freeing you.'

'You'll *consider* it?'

'Have you forgotten already that I hold all the cards here?' He sauntered back and stopped in front of her.

Suddenly, Ruby wished she'd stayed put in the middle of the bed. *This* close the heat emanating from his satin-like skin blanketed her. The urge to move her fingers just that little bit and touch the skin covering his ribcage was immense.

'Go ahead,' he invited softly. Silkily.

Flames leapt through her bloodstream. 'Excuse me?'

'You want to touch me. Go ahead. We can pick up this conversation in a moment once you've satisfied your craving.'

'I… You're wrong. I don't want to touch you. There's no craving. What I want is to be set free—'

Her words froze when he placed large hands on her hips and pulled her into his body.

'Well, despite you ruining my evening, I *still* have a craving for you.'

He smothered her protests by capturing her mouth again. It was as potent as before but this time there was a rough demand in his kiss that spoke of his fury beneath all that outward calm.

But rough didn't mean less pleasurable. Her lips parted, welcoming the jagged thrust of his tongue and the domineering pressure of his kiss.

She moaned before she could stop herself, flexing fingers that wouldn't obey their order to stay put, and touching the velvety smoothness of his neck and collarbone.

By the time he lifted his head, they were both panting. He slowly licked his lips, savouring her taste. The sight of his wet tongue sent liquid fire straight to that raging hunger between her thighs.

Ruby shut her eyes in shuddering despair and opened them to find him sliding off her shoes.

'God, will you please stop doing things like that?' she snapped.

'I'm into kinky when the occasion calls for it, but I don't generally risk puncturing a lung with stiletto heels unless the payback is worth it.' He flung her shoes away. 'Do you need help with your dress?'

'No! Why on earth would I want that?' She edged away from him, the fear that her emotions wouldn't be as easy to control around this man spiking through her.

'It's nearly two a.m. And we're yet to have our little tête-à-tête. But if you want to keep cutting off your circulation in that restricting dress, suit yourself. Tell me why you're here,' he bit out, as if he wanted to be done with the conversation.

'Release me first,' she insisted.

'I released you three minutes ago.'

Shocked, Ruby glanced down at her wrists. Sure enough, the velvet rope was loose enough to free herself. She'd been too spellbound by his kiss to notice.

She met his hard, mocking gaze. Rubbing her right wrist, she encountered his watch. She pulled it off and held it out to him.

He didn't take it. 'I'm waiting for an answer.'

'My name is Ruby Trevelli.'

He continued to stare at her. 'Should that mean anything to me?'

Despite knowing how self-absorbed he was, that flippant question hurt. She flung his watch on the bed. He calmly retrieved it, took hold of her wrist, slipped it back on, and returned to his predator-like position.

'What—?'

'Answer me. Should your name mean anything to me?'

'Yes. I was recently voted Élite Chef.'

His lips twisted. 'My apologies. I don't keep up with pop culture,' he said.

'Well, you should. Your TV company sponsored the show.'

He frowned. 'I have over sixty media companies scattered

all over the world. It would be impossible to keep up with every progamme that's aired through my networks. So you're here to collect some sort of prize—is that it?' The disappointment she'd heard earlier was back, accompanied this time by a flash of weariness that disappeared as quickly as it'd arrived.

'You make it sound like a whimsical endeavour. I assure you, it's not.'

'Enlighten me, then, Miss Contest Winner. Why have you flown thousands of miles to accost me?'

Put like that it *did* sound whimsical. Except this was her life and livelihood they were talking about, the independent life she'd worked hard for so she wouldn't be pulled into her parents' damaging orbit. The life that was being threatened by a loan shark.

'I want your company to honour its agreement and pay me what I'm owed.'

His face hardened into a taut, formidable mask of disdain. 'You came after me because of *money?*' His sneer had thickened.

Ruby couldn't really dwell on that. She needed to state her purpose and leave this room, this suite. He was close, so tantalisingly close, the warmth of his skin and the spicy scent of his aftershave made stringing words together an increasingly difficult task. He smelled like heaven. And she wanted to drown in it.

'Prize money, yes.'

His eyes narrowed. 'But why come after me? Why not go after the man I've put in place to head NMC?'

'You think I haven't tried? No one would take my calls.'

'Really? No one in a company with over a thousand employees?'

'No. Trust me, I have the phone bill to prove it.'

'Well, clearly, I need to hire better staff.'

'I don't like your tone,' Ruby snapped. She sidled towards the edge of the bed.

He caught her and placed her back in front of him, keeping her captive with one large hand on her waist.

'What tone do you mean?' Silver eyes gleamed with cynical amusement.

With every breath she took, the imprint of his hand seared her skin. 'You obviously don't believe me. Why would I travel thousands of miles unless it was because I'd hit a brick wall?'

'Or you'd hoped an extra tight dress and body that won't quit would get you an even better deal?'

The image his words conjured up made blood leach from her face. It was one she'd vowed never to portray. 'I understand you don't know me, Mr Valentino, but I've never used sex or my sexuality to further my career. You can be as offensive and as delusional as you want. The simple fact is Nigel Stone never took my call in the two dozen times I tried to reach him.'

His eyes narrowed at her furious words but he kept silent.

'We can resolve this very quickly. Call him now, get him to talk to me. Then I'll get out of your hair.'

'It's Saturday morning back in the States. I make it a point never to disturb my employees during the weekend.'

Anger stiffened her spine. 'Yeah, right.'

His cynical smile widened. 'You don't believe me?'

'I believe you do exactly what you want when you want. If it suited you, you'd be on the phone right now.'

His shrug outlined sleek muscle beneath his skin. He moved with an innate grace that made Ruby's pulse race shamefully. 'Fine. I admit I ride my employees hard when I have to. But I also recognise their need for down time the same way I recognise the need for mine.'

'You're telling me you need your beauty sleep to function?' she snapped.

'Down time doesn't necessarily mean sleep, *amante*. Tonight, I was counting on wild, unfettered sex,' he delivered smoothly.

She flung herself away from him, from the temptation his words dredged up inside her, before that Trevelli gene she so feared could be fully activated.

Far too often since she'd clapped eyes on him, she'd found herself imagining what sex would be like. Her roommate had referred to the best sex as sheet-clawing, toe-curling. At the time Ruby had silently scoffed at how anything besides the best, decadently prepared dessert would feel that great.

Now she couldn't stop herself from wondering...

Disgust at herself propelled her off the bed. She refused to sink into the quagmire of rampant promiscuity.

Her feet hit the luxurious carpet, bringing a much-needed return to reality. She darted out of the door and hurried along the long hallway towards the main suite doors.

With relief, she grasped the door handle and yanked it down. Nothing happened. She pulled harder.

Glancing around wildly, she spotted the electronic panel and pressed the most obvious-looking button.

Nothing.

'You can't get out unless I allow you out.'

She whirled. He casually leaned one shoulder against the hallway wall. The sight of him standing there, looking sexily tousled and half naked, made panic flare anew inside her.

'Then let me out.'

'I could. But once I do, any hope of a discussion about why you're here ends. My company, if it's liable as you say, owes you nothing the minute you walk out of here.'

'That's preposterous! I signed a contract. *You* signed a contract. You can't just back out on a whim.'

'Think about it, Ruby. You've travelled thousands of miles to get my attention. I intend to give you that attention. Do you think it prudent to walk out now, when you could be so close?'

'I...' She sucked in a breath as overwhelming feelings swamped her. 'Why can't we discuss it now?'

'Because I don't like to discuss business without a clear head. And since you've plied me with exquisite cocktails all evening, I'd be making those decisions under severe influence.' He tilted his head again in that alarmingly endearing way and a lock of hair fell over his eyes.

Dear God. This man was truly lethal. He oozed sex and sensuality without so much as lifting a finger.

'You didn't ply me with all those drinks in order to take advantage of me, did you? Because that would be horrifyingly disappointing.'

Outraged, she gasped. 'I most certainly did not.'

Slowly, he extended a hand to her. 'In that case, Ruby Trevelli, there's no earthly reason not to stay. Is there?'

Narciso was doing his best to stop his fury from showing. The same way he was doing his best to keep from kicking himself for ignoring the alarm bells.

Usually he could spot chancers and gold-diggers a mile away, be they tuxedo-clad or dressed in designer gowns that looked too small for them.

For a moment he wished she'd kept her mouth shut until after he'd slept with her to make her avarice known. He would've been a lot more generous than he was feeling now.

He would also have felt used.

Fury mounted and his frustrated erection threatened to cut him in half as she stayed out of his reach. Out of his arms.

Recalling her responsiveness, the gut-clenching potency of her kiss, he nearly growled.

She kissed as if she were born for it. Narciso wondered how many men she'd kissed like that in the past and felt a red haze wash over his fury.

Dio, what was wrong with him? He should find the nearest phone and report her to management.

Zeus, his host and owner of the club, had so far excelled in keeping people like Ruby away from *Q Virtus* guests. Sure, most *Petit Qs* would accept a generous gift from a guest, but blatant stalking wasn't tolerated.

Except, his stalker seemed eager to get *away* from him, her catlike blue eyes apprehensive as she glanced at his outstretched hand.

'Come here,' he commanded.

She swayed towards him, then abruptly halted her forward momentum. 'If you're too drunk to talk, what other reason is there for me to stay? And don't mention wild sex. Because that's not going to happen.'

Contrary to what he'd said, his mind was as clear and as sharp as a fillet knife. And it sensed a curious dichotomy in her words and actions. The dress, make-up and screw-me stilettos said one thing. Her words indicated another.

He intended to burrow until he found the truth.

Nice choice of words, Narciso, he thought as arousal spiked higher in his blood. Lowering his hand, he turned abruptly.

'I'm returning to the bedroom. If you're not there within the next minute, I'll take it that our business is concluded,' he said over his shoulder.

'Wait! You can't do that...'

Narciso smiled with satisfaction at her frustration. Whether she followed him or not, there was no way he was letting her out of his suite tonight. Not until he'd had her checked out thoroughly and satisfied himself what sort of threat she posed.

He recalled the circumstances of their meeting. Of all the tables she could've been hostessing, she'd been at Giacomo's table.

This time he didn't ignore the churning in his gut. Giacomo had played that game before...

He turned and found her two steps behind him but any satisfaction was marred by the new set of questions clamouring for answers.

'Why are you really here, Ruby? Did the old man send you?'

Fresh trepidation flared in her eyes at his harsh tone. 'Who... Oh, that guy you were playing with? No, I have no idea who he is and I'd never met him before tonight.'

He tried to read her. Surely, even seasoned liars couldn't look him straight in the eye as she was without flinching?

'Be warned, if I find that to be untrue, there'll be hell to pay.'

'I'm telling you, I don't know him.' Her fingers meshed together and she began to fidget. But not once did her stare waver from his.

Narciso decided to be satisfied. For now. He entered the bedroom and crossed to the en suite.

'So I'm here. Now what?' she asked.

'I'm going to take a shower. You do whatever you want. As long as you don't leave this room.'

'God, this is nuts,' he heard her mutter as he entered the bathroom. Despite the volatile emotions churning through him, he smiled. From the corner of his eye, he watched her head once more to the stunning view of Macau City.

Silhouetted against the view, her body was so perfectly stunning, his mouth dried. Disappointment welled in his chest but he suppressed it as he undressed.

The cold shower was bracing enough to calm his arousal but not enough to wash away the bitterness as he replayed his evening.

Giacomo was bent on trying to take Narciso down.

Well, that suited Narciso fine. Although Narciso could've destroyed him with that last move, the notion of leaving him dangling a little bit longer had been irresistible.

The opportunity would present itself again soon enough. Giacomo was predictable in his hatred for him, if for nothing else.

And at thirty, exactly ten years after his father's most cutting betrayal, the need for vengeance burned just as brightly in Narciso's veins.

For as long as he'd been old enough to retain his memories, Narciso had known that Giacomo bore him a deep, abiding hatred. As a child he'd been bewildered as to why nothing he did pleased or satisfied the man he once called Papa.

On his eleventh birthday, a whisky-soaked Giacomo had finally revealed to him the reason he detested the sight of his son. At first, even reeling from the shock of the discovery, Narciso had stupidly believed he could turn things around, make his father, if not love him, at least learn to cohabit peacefully with him. He'd made sure his grades were perfect, that he was quiet and obedient and exemplary in all things.

Narciso's mouth twisted. That had lasted all of a year before he'd accepted he was flogging a dead horse. When his thirteenth birthday had come and gone without so much as a single lit candle on a store-bought birthday cake, he'd finally admitted that war was the only way forward.

He'd suppressed whatever heartache had threatened to catch him unawares in the dead of night and used animosity to feed his ambitions to succeed. He'd won scholarships to the best colleges in the world. His head for figures had seen him attain his first million by eighteen. By twenty he'd been a multi-millionaire.

Twenty…also the age he'd met Maria, the unexpected tool his father had used against him. The wound gaped another inch.

With a sharp curse, he shut off the shower. Snapping up a towel, he tied it around his waist.

Maria was dead to him, but, in a way, he was pleased for her transient presence in his life ten years ago. She'd reinforced his belief that lowering his guard, even for a moment, was fool-hardy. That even fake love came at a steep price.

Money and sex were the two things he thrived on now. Emotions…connections, hell, *love,* were a complete waste of his time.

He entered the bedroom and found Ruby reclining on the bed, legs crossed, one bare foot tapping in agitation. She shot upright at his entry. After that one quick look, Narciso barely glanced in her direction as he walked to the connecting dressing room.

The whole evening was screwed up. His thwarted efforts to bed her, and now his unexplained trip down memory lane had left him in an edgy mood. Snatching at his fast-dwindling control, he reached for the rarely used silk pajama bottoms and dropped his towel.

The choking sound made him glance over his shoulder through the open door. She sat frozen on the bed, her eyes wide with astonishment.

'Something wrong?' he asked as he stabbed one leg into the garment. At her silence, he started to turn.

She shut her eyes and jerked away from him. He pulled the bottoms on and entered the bedroom. 'Open your eyes. It's safe to look now.'

She opened her eyes but kept her gaze averted.

'Come on, now, the way you're acting you'd think I was the first naked male you'd ever seen.'

That gurgling sound came again and Narciso shook his head. 'I have very little interest in virgins, *amante*. If you hope to snag my attention, I suggest you drop that particular act.'

She inhaled sharply. 'It's not an—' She bit off the rest of her answer as he drew back the sheets.

Four of the six pillows he threw to the floor before he got in. The sight of her sitting so stiffly made his jaw tighten. Reaching across, he pulled her into the middle and pulled the sheet over them.

'You were saying?'

She shook her head. 'Nothing. Are you really going to sleep?'

'Yes. I suggest you get some sleep too even though I fear for your circulation in that dress you're wearing.'

'I'm fine.'

'If you say so.' He relaxed against the pillows. Sleep would be elusive with her so close. For a moment he wondered why he was torturing himself like this.

Keep your friends close and your stalkers closer?

He suppressed a grim smile, grabbed the remote and doused the light in the bedroom. But with one sensory factor taken away, her erratic breathing became amplified.

Good. If he was to be tortured with images of what sex between them would be like, it was only fair she experienced the same fate.

'What happens tomorrow?' she asked quietly.

'Tomorrow we talk. And by talk I mean you come clean, completely, as to why you're here. Because if you hold anything back from me, I won't hesitate to throw you to the wolves.'

CHAPTER FIVE

RUBY WOKE WITH the distinct feeling that something had changed. It took a millisecond to realise what that *something* was.

'You took my clothes off?' she screeched, her fingers flying to the hem of the black T-shirt that had miraculously appeared on her body.

The man who lay so languidly beside her, his head propped up on his hand, nodded.

'I feared you'd suffocate in your sleep in that dress. Despite your dubious reasons for being here, even I would find it difficult to explain death by designer gown to the authorities. You were quite co-operative. I think it was the only time you've been co-operative since we reached my suite, which tells me you were as uncomfortable as I suspected.'

She licked her lips and struggled not to squirm under his scrutiny. At least her bra and panties were intact. But the fact was she didn't recall what had happened. And there was only one worrying explanation for that. 'I was tired,' she bluffed.

'Right.' Silver eyes bore into her until she felt like a fly hooked on a pin.

His gaze dropped to her twisting fingers, and she abruptly stilled the movement. 'Tell me what happened. *Exactly.*'

One brow rose at her firm directive but Ruby was desperate to know what had happened during the night. She'd tossed and turned in agitation until sheer exhaustion had finally pulled her under some time before dawn.

'You tried to escape a few times. I brought you back to bed.'

God. No. It'd happened again...

Definitely time to leave. She tried to move, and felt a snag on her foot. Shoving aside tangled sheets, she stared in horror at the rope tied around her ankle.

'You tied me up again! Do you have a thing for bondage?'

His eyes gleamed. 'Until last night, I'd never needed to tie a woman to keep her with me.'

'Oh, well, lucky me. Did you tie me before or after you took off my dress?'

'After the second time you tried to take the door off its hinges to make your escape, we came back here and I relieved you of your suicidal gown and put the T-shirt on—' A deep frown slashed his face. 'Are you saying you don't remember any of this?'

She sucked in a slow breath and looked away.

He caught her chin in his hand and forced her to look at him, his steady gaze demanding an answer. '*Dio,* you really don't remember?'

Ruby had no choice but to come clean. 'No. sometimes I... sleepwalk.'

His brows hit his hairline. 'You *sleepwalk?* How often is sometimes?'

'Not for a while, to my knowledge. It only happens when I'm...distressed.'

His frown intensified. 'You found last night distressing?'

'Being tied up and kept prisoner? No, that was a picnic in the park.' She tugged at her ankle restraint. 'And now I'm tied up again.'

'It was for your own good. After I put the restraint on, you stopped making a run for it. I think secretly you liked it.' His fingers caressed along her jaw, his eyes lowering to her lips.

Instantly the mood changed, thickened with sensual promise. 'I'm *not* into bondage.' Or sex with playboys, or anyone for that matter!

'How do you know? Have you ever tried it?'

'No. But I've never jumped off a cliff either, and I'm certain I wouldn't enjoy that experience.'

'Fair point. For the record, I have. With the right equipment, all experiences can be extremely enjoyable. Exhilarating even.'

She watched, terrified and mesmerised, as his head started to lower. 'What are you doing?'

'I'm kissing you *bon giornu, bedda*. Relax.'

That was easier said than done when every nerve in her body was strained in anticipation of the touch of his mouth on hers. She told herself she was sluggish because she was sleep deprived. But it was a lie.

As much as she yearned to deny it, she wanted the pressure of his demanding kiss and the heady racing of her blood through her veins.

His moan as he deepened the kiss echoed the piercing need inside her.

One hand clamped on her hip, drew her sideways into him. At the sensation of his sleep-warmed body against hers, she moaned. The fact that she was clothed from neck to hip and he was clothed from hip to ankle didn't alter the stormy sensation of their bodies meshing together.

Nipples, stung to life at the touch of his mouth on hers, peaked and ached as they brushed his chest.

When his hand moved under the T-shirt and skimmed over her panties, Ruby jerked at the vicious punch of desire that threatened to flatten her.

She was drowning. And she didn't want to be rescued.

'*Dio mio,* you're addictive, *bedda,*' he murmured against her mouth before plunging back in. His tongue shot between her lips to slide against hers. He staked his claim on her until she couldn't think straight. Even when his mouth left hers to nibble along her jaw, she strained closer, her hand sliding up his chest in a bold caress that shocked and thrilled her at the same time.

When her nail grazed his nipple, he hissed. Stunned at the surge of power that action gave her, she flicked her nail again.

'Careful, *amante,* or I might have to repay the kindness.'

Lost in a swirl of desire, she barely heeded the warning. Bringing up her other hand between them, she flicked both flat nipples at once.

'*Maledizione!*' He pushed her back onto the bed and yanked up her T-shirt.

Danger shrieked in her head a second before his mouth closed over her nipple. Tonguing, licking, he pulled the willing flesh deep into his mouth.

Sensation as she'd never felt before tore through her. Between her legs where her need burned fiercest, liquid heat fuelled her raging desire.

Her fingers curled up and spiked into his hair as he transferred his attention to her other nipple. A little rougher than before, he used his teeth this time.

Her tiny scream echoed through the bedroom as her head slammed back against the pillow.

Feeling his thick arousal against her thigh, she moved her leg, eager to rub closer against the potent evidence of his need.

The snap of the ankle rope broke through her haze. The reality of what she was doing hit Ruby with the force of a two-by-four.

'No!' She pushed at his shoulders until he lifted his head. The sight of her nipples, reddened and wet from his ministrations, made dismay slither through her in equal measures. She was nothing like her parents. Nothing—

'What's wrong, *bedda?*' he grated huskily.

'What's wrong? Everything!'

'Everything is a huge undertaking. Narrow it down for me a little. I'll take care of it.'

She pushed harder. 'For a start. Get. Off. Me.'

His nostrils flared with displeasure and his fingers bit into her hip. 'You were moaning your willingness a moment ago.'

'Thankfully, I've come to my senses. Get off me and take off that…shackle you've placed on my ankle.'

He slowly levered himself off her but not before she got

another sensation of his thick arousal. Flames rushed up her cheeks.

Back in his previous position, he dropped his gaze from hers to her breasts. Realising she was still exposed, she yanked her bra cups into place and tugged down the T-shirt. A T-shirt that bore his unique scent, which chose that moment to wash over her again. As if she weren't suffering enough.

'I don't like women who blow hot and cold, *tesoro*.'

'Where I come from a woman still has the right to say no.'

'A stance I fully respect. Except your actions and your words are at direct variance with each other. You crave me almost as much as I crave you. I can only conclude that this is a ploy to string me along until I'm too whipped to put up much protest against your demands.'

Again his description of her behaviour struck painfully close to the bone, pushing all her fears to the fore. Struggling to hide it, she raised an eyebrow.

'Wow, you really have a low opinion of yourself, don't you? Or is that a high opinion on my sexual prowess?'

'Unlike you, I'm not afraid to admit my desire for you. It's almost enough to tempt me to tell you to name your price so we can be done with this...*aperitivo* and get to the main course.' There was a hard bite to his voice that instinctively warned her to do that would be a mistake.

'I only want you to hear me out. You said we'd talk this morning.'

He got up from the bed in a sleek, graceful move that brought to mind a jungle creature.

The unmistakable evidence of his arousal when he faced her made her swallow. He showed no embarrassment in his blatant display of manhood. Even in thwarted desire, Narciso Valentino wore his male confidence with envy-inducing ease. Whereas she remained cowering beneath the sheets, afraid of the sensual waves threatening to drown her.

'And so we will. Come through to the kitchen. Caffeine is a

poor substitute for sex but it'll have to do.' With that pithy pro-
nouncement, he walked out of the bedroom.

She lay there, floundering in a sea of panic and confusion.
If anyone had told her she'd be in Narciso Valentino's bed mere
hours after meeting him, she'd have laughed herself hoarse. Particularly since she'd vowed never to mix business with pleasure
after what had happened with Simon.

But what Narciso had roused in her just now had frightened
and excited her. Kissing him had been holding a live, dangerous
firework in the palm of her hand. She hadn't been sure whether
she would experience the most spectacular show of lights or
blow herself to smithereens with it.

And yet she'd been almost desolate when the kiss ended.
Which showed how badly things could get out of hand.

Squeezing her eyes shut, she counted to ten. The earlier she
finished her business with Narciso and got on the plane back
to New York, the better.

Throwing off the sheet, she glanced at the velvet rope around
her ankle. Twisting her body into the appropriate position, she
tugged on the double knot, surprised when it came loose easily.

Again, the realisation that she could've freed herself at any
time made her view of him alter a little. Her fingers lingered
on the rope warmed from her body.

Bondage sex. Until now, the scenario had never even crossed
her mind. But suddenly, the thought of being tied down while
Narciso laid her inhibitions to waste took up centre stage in
her mind.

Heat flaming her whole body, she jumped from the bed. Upright, his T-shirt reached well past her knees, and covered her
arms to her elbows.

She glanced at her gown, laid carefully over the arm of the
chaise longue, and made up her mind. She would dress after
they'd had their talk. She couldn't bear being restrained in the
too-tight dress just yet. Ditto for her heels.

Stilettos and a T-shirt in the presence of a dangerously sexual man like Narciso Valentino evoked an image she didn't want to tempt into life now, or ever.

For some reason, her body turned him on. She wasn't stupid enough to bait the lion more than he was already baited.

Barefoot, she left the bedroom and went in search of the kitchen.

He stood at a centre island in a kitchen that made the chef in her want to weep with envy. State-of-the-art equipment lined the surfaces and walls and through a short alcove a floor-to-ceiling wine rack displayed exquisite vintages.

'You get all this for a two-day stay?'

He jerked at her question. Before he could cover his emotions, Ruby glimpsed a painfully bleak look in his eyes.

A second later, the look was gone as he shrugged. 'It suits my needs.'

'Your needs... I'd kill for a kitchen like this in my restaurant.'

'You own a restaurant?' he asked.

She concluded her survey of the appliances and faced him. 'Not yet. I would've been on my way to opening Dolce Italia by now if NMC had honoured its commitments.'

'Ah, the sins of imaginary corporate sharks.'

The coffee machine finished going through its wake-up motions. He pressed a button and the beans started to churn.

'Not imaginary.' Ruby stepped forward when she realised what he was doing. 'Wait, you're doing it wrong. We're in a warm climate. The coffee beans expand in warm weather so you need to grind them looser to extract the maximum taste. Here let me do it.' Even though stepping closer would bring her dangerously close to his sleek frame, she seized the opportunity to make herself useful and not just stare at his broad, naked back. A back she could suddenly picture herself clawing in the heat of desire.

Just as she tried not to stare when he leaned his hip against the counter and crossed his arms over his bare chest.

'How are you at multitasking?' he asked.

'It's essential in my line of business.' Content with the setting, she pressed the button to resume the grinding and went to the fridge. She grabbed the creamer, and forced herself not to gape at the mouth-watering ingredients in there.

'Good, then you can talk while you prepare the coffee. Tell me everything I need to know.' His brisk tone was all business.

Quickly, she summarised the events of the past two months.

'So you entered this competition as a chef?' he asked.

'Yes, I have a degree in hospitality management and a diploma in gourmet cuisine and I'm an approved board-certified mixologist.'

He grinned. 'You have to go to college to mix drinks?'

'You have to go to school to wash dishes right these days or someone will sue your ass.' She started to grin, then stopped herself. 'I mean…if you don't want to be sued for accidentally poisoning someone. Besides, I plan to make my cocktail bar accessible to allergy-sufferers, too, so I need to know what I'm doing.'

'Which of your drinks is your favourite?' he fired back.

The question threw her for a second. Then she shrugged. 'They're all my favourite.'

'Describe the taste of your signature drink,' he pressed.

She went in search of coffee cups, opening several cabinets before she located them. She had to reach up to grab them and the cool air that passed over the backs of her legs reminded her how exposed she was.

'Umm, I don't actually like cocktails that much,' she blurted to distract herself from her state of undress.

'You're a mixologist who doesn't like her own creations? How do you know you're not poisoning the general population?'

'Because nobody's died yet sampling my drinks. And as to how I know my drinks rock? I try them out on my roommate.'

'You want me to invest…how much does my company owe you?'

'Two hundred thousand dollars to help towards construction and advertising costs for Dolce Italia.'

'Right, two hundred thousand dollars, based on your room-mate's assessment of your talent?'

She poured and passed him a cup, forcing herself not to react to the spark of electricity when their fingers brushed. 'You threw away thirty million last night without blinking but you're grilling me over two hundred thousand?'

He stiffened. 'That was different.' His voice held icy warning.

She heeded it. *'Anyway,'* she hurried on, 'thousands of people voted for me to win *your* show based on three of my best dishes and cocktails.'

His gaze drifted over her, lingered at her breasts then down her legs before he came back to her face. 'Are you sure that's the only reason they voted?'

The sudden tremble in her fingers made her set the cup down. 'You're an ass for making that inference.' Again, much too close to home. Too many times her mother had been ridiculed for using her sexuality to boost ratings, a fact Ruby had burned with humiliation for every single time.

'What inference?' he asked with a sly grin.

'The stupid sexist one you're making. Are you saying they voted for me because I have boobs?' Her rough accusation finally got his attention. The smile slid from his face but not the stark hunger in his eyes.

'Very nice ones.'

Despite her annoyance, heat rushed through her. 'Yeah, well, two of the other contestants had boobs, too.'

'I have no interest in theirs,' he returned blandly.

She picked up her cup and started to blow on her coffee, noticed his intense gaze on her mouth and thought better of it. 'Are you really that shallow?'

'Sì, I am.'

'No, you're not.'

'You wound me.'

'You wound yourself. You're clearly intelligent—'

'Grazie—'

'Or you wouldn't be worth billions. I fail to see why you feel the need to add this to the equation.'

'Tell me, sweet Ruby, why is it sexist to state that I appreciate an attractive body when I see it?'

Her mouth tightened. 'It's sexist when you imply I got where I am by flaunting it when you couldn't be more wrong.'

'Point taken.' He said nothing further.

'Is that supposed to be an apology?'

'Yes, I apologise unreservedly for making observations about your body.'

'That's almost as bad as saying "I apologise if your feelings are hurt" instead of "I'm sorry for hurting your feelings".'

'Let's not dwell on the pedantic. You have my unreserved apologies.' His gaze was steady and clear.

Ruby chose to believe he meant it. 'Thank you.'

'Good. I tried to reach Stone. I've been informed he's on vacation and can't be reached.'

She took a huge gulp of coffee and nearly groaned at the superb taste. Then his words broke through. 'Right. I wasn't born yesterday, you know.'

The seriously gorgeous grin returned. 'I know, and I'm very grateful for that.'

'Get to the point, *please*.'

'Stone is trekking in the Amazon for the next three weeks.'

Alarm skated through her. 'I can't wait another three weeks. I'll lose everything I've poured into getting the restaurant off the ground so far.'

'Which is what exactly?'

'Simon secured the rent but I put up my own money for the conversion of the space and the catering equipment.'

He froze. 'Who is Simon?' he asked in a silky tone threaded with steel.

'My ex-business partner.'

'Enlighten me why he's your ex,' he said in that abrupt, imperious way she'd come to expect.

The ache from Simon's betrayal flared anew. 'We didn't see eye to eye so we parted ways.'

Narciso's eyes narrowed. 'Was he your lover?'

She hesitated. 'Almost,' she finally admitted. 'We met in college, but lost touch for a while. A year ago we met again in New York. I told him about opening my restaurant and he offered to become my partner. We got close…'

He tensed. 'But?'

'But he neglected to tell me he had a pregnant wife at home and…I almost slept with him. He almost made me an accomplice in his infidelity.' The thought sent cold anger through her.

'How did you find out?'

Her hand tightened around her coffee cup. 'We were on our way to Connecticut for a romantic getaway when his wife called to say she'd gone into labour. I trusted him, and he turned out to be no better than…' She shook her head angrily and jumped when his fingers touched hers. Looking up, her eyes connected with his surprisingly gentle ones.

'I think you'll agree he takes the douche-bag crown, no?'

She swallowed the lump in her throat. 'Yes.'

He remained silent for several minutes, then he drained his cup. 'So my company's contribution is to help finish your restaurant?'

'That and the advertising costs for the first six months.'

'Do you have any paperwork?'

'Not with me, no. I couldn't exactly bring a briefcase to the job last night. But Nigel can prove it…'

'I'm taking over from Nigel,' he said abruptly.

'Excuse me?'

He set his cup down. 'As of now, I've relieved him of his duty to you. You'll now deal with me and me alone.'

That felt a little too…sudden… Ruby assured herself it was the reason why her heartbeat had suddenly escalated. She refused to let hope rise until she'd read the small print in his words. 'So…you'll sign over what NMC promised me?'

His eyes gleamed as he regarded her. 'Eventually,' he said lazily.

'Ah, there it is. The big, fat catch. What does *eventually* mean?' she demanded.

'I need proof that you're as good as you say you are. I don't endorse mediocre ventures.'

'Wow, are you always this insulting in the morning?'

'Sexual frustration doesn't sit well with any man, *amante,* least of all me.'

'And you think bringing your sexual frustration into a business discussion is appropriate?'

Silver eyes impaled her where she stood. 'You followed me thousands of miles and inveigled yourself into my company under false pretenses. You wish to discuss who holds the monopoly on what's appropriate right now?'

'What other choice did I have? I couldn't lose everything I've worked for because your employee is chasing orangutans in the Amazon.'

'I may be way off the mark but I don't think there are any orangutans in the Amazon. Borneo, on the other hand—'

'I didn't mean it literally. I meant...' She sighed. 'Bottom line is, NMC agreed to help me launch my business and it's reneging on the deal.'

'And I'm giving you a chance to get things back on track.'

'By making me jump through even more hoops?'

'I employ the best people. There must be a reason why Stone delayed in honouring the agreement.'

'And you think the fault is mine?' Irritation bristled under her skin. He stood there, arrogant and nonchalant as she flailed against the emotional and professional sands shifting under her feet.

'I'm trying to meet you in the middle.'

'All you have to do is review the show's footage. There were world-renowned food critics who judged my cuisine and cocktails the best. I won fair and square.'

'So you keep saying. And yet I'm wondering if there's something else going on here. If everything was above board, why didn't you use lawyers to hold my company to account? Why the very personal touch?'

'I don't have the kind of money it takes to involve lawyers. Besides, I was hoping you'd be reasonable.'

He moved towards her, his gaze pinned on her face. Danger blazed from his eyes. Along with hunger, passion and a need to win at all costs.

Her heart hammered as she forced herself to return his stare.

'You lied in order to get close to me. And you continued to lie until we were alone together. Having caught a glimpse of who I am, Ruby, how reasonable do you think I am?' His tone was silky soft, but she wasn't fooled. Underneath the lethally thrilling charm and the man who'd shown a surprising gentle side moments ago lay a ruthless mogul who ate amateurs for breakfast.

During her internet trawl she'd come across his moniker— The Warlock of Wall Street.

It took a special kind of genius to reach multibillionaire status by twenty-five and even more to attain the kind of wealth and influence Narciso Valentino wielded by his thirtieth birthday. If she didn't tread carefully, she'd leave Macau the same way she'd arrived—with nothing.

'I'm not unwilling to renegotiate our terms, Mr Valentino...' she ventured.

'I've had my mouth on parts of your body that I believe have earned me the right to hear you say my first name.'

Her blush was fierce and horrifyingly embarrassing. 'Fine! You can have thirty per cent,' she blurted.

His eyebrows shot up. 'Thirty per cent of your body?'

'What are you talking about? God, you think I'm renegotiating with my *body*?' She gasped in shocked horror. 'I'll have you know that I'd rather *die* than do something like that!'

His discomfiture was evident as he slowly straightened and spiked a hand through his hair. 'I'm...sorry,' he murmured.

A touch of warmth dispelled the ice. 'Apology accepted.'

'*Per favore,* enlighten me as to what you meant.'

'Part of the deal for winning was that you'd help with the cash prize and advertising and I'd give you a twenty-five-per-cent share in my business for the first three years. After that I'd have the option to buy it back from you. I'm willing to go up to thirty per cent.'

His shook his head. 'I have a new proposal for you. Agree to it and you can keep your extra five per cent.'

'Do I have a choice?'

'There's always a choice, *cara.*'

'Okay, let's hear it.'

'Convince me of your talent. If you're good enough, I'll hire you to cater my upcoming VIP party. If you're better than good, I'll recommend you to a few people. Now, the only thing you need to decide is if it's a choice you wish for yourself.'

'But I've already proved I deserve this by winning the show.'

'Then this should be a doozy.' He raised an eyebrow. 'Do you agree to my terms?'

The sense of injustice burned within her, the need to stand her ground and demand her due strong.

But from what she'd seen of him so far he could destroy her just as easily as he'd offered to help her. He'd rightly pointed out that she'd sought him out under false pretences. She should be thanking her lucky stars he hadn't turned her over to the security guards.

The small print in her *Petit Q* contract had warned of serious repercussions if she breached confidentiality or behaved inappropriately towards a *Q Virtus* member.

So far she'd breached several of those guidelines. It was therefore in her interest to stay on the right side of Narciso Valentino.

If he could throw away thirty million dollars with the careless flick of those elegant fingers, surely it was worth her while to endure this small sacrifice to prove herself to Narciso. Getting her restaurant opening back on track would also send her parents the message once and for all that she had no intention of bowing to their pressure to join the family business.

She sucked in a breath, which hopelessly stalled when his eyes darkened. 'Yes, I agree to your terms.'

He didn't move. He just stood there staring at her. Ruby had the weird sensation he was weighing her up, judging her...

Unable to stand his stare, she started to turn away. His eyes dropped to her bare legs, heat flaring in his gaze. The power of it was so forceful she took a step back. Then another.

'Stop,' he rasped.

'Why?'

'I need you.'

Her heart hammered. 'What?'

His nostrils flared as he reached and captured her arm. Strong fingers slid down her elbow to her wrist. Ruby's pulse raced harder under the pressure of his fingers as he raised her right arm.

The electronic beep as he activated the smartwatch on her wrist knocked her out of her lust haze. Biting the inside of her cheek to bring her down to reality worked for a few seconds, until he started to speak.

Sicilian wasn't in any way similar to the language she'd learnt growing up, but she managed to pick up a few words that had her frowning.

'You're not returning to New York?'

'Not yet. My plan was to take a long-needed vacation after Macau.'

Her heart sank. 'So I still have to wait until you come to New York to finalise this agreement.'

'Not at all, Ruby. I leave for Belize tonight. And you're com-ing with me.'

The sight of her open-mouthed was almost amusing. Almost. Had he not been caught up in the maelstrom of severely thwarted desire, Narciso would've laughed at her expression.

As it was, he couldn't see beyond the need to experience again the sensational taste of those lips.

Pure sin. Wrapped in sweet, angelic deliciousness.

He'd never kissed lips like hers. Or tasted nipples like hers. In fact, so far Ruby Trevelli was proving disconcertingly unique in all aspects. Even the confession of her bastard of an ex's betrayal had touched him in a way he most definitely did not desire.

The flash of pain he'd seen had made his insides clench with an alien emotion that had set even more alarm bells clanging.

He hadn't intended to go to Belize till after the party he'd planned for when his Russian deal was completed.

But he was nothing if not adaptable.

'Belize?' Astonishment blazed from her stunning blue eyes.

'Yes. I have a yacht moored there. We'll sail around along the coast, dive in the Blue Hole. And in between, you'll stun me with your culinary delights. But be warned, nothing short of perfection will satisfy me.'

'I've never provided anything short of that. But...' She hesitated, again displaying that reticence he'd sensed in her earlier. If she wanted to play hard to get, she was going about it the right way. He wanted her...hard. But he was no pushover.

'But what?'

'We need to agree on one thing.' Her pulse throbbed under his thumb. He wanted to stop himself from caressing the silky, delicate skin but he couldn't help himself.

'Sì?'

'From now on things remain strictly business between us. The next time we have a discussion, I'd rather do it without the need for ropes.'

The hard tug of arousal the image brought almost made him groan out loud. 'I guarantee you, *amante,* the next time I tie you up, it'll be because you beg me to.'

She snatched her wrist from his grasp.

'Okay. And Superman rides on a unicorn, right?'

'I have no idea about that. Ropes, on the other hand—'

'Will play no part in our interaction for the duration I'm to prove myself to you. Unless, of course, you're bringing your girlfriend along. In which case, what you get up to with her is your business.'

Irritation fizzed inside him. Having the attraction he knew she reciprocated dismissed so casually stuck like a barb under his skin. 'I'm currently unattached. But I don't think I'll stay that way for much longer,' he said.

Her eyes widened but her lips pursed. Again arousal bit deep.

Suddenly, he wanted to leave Macau. Wanted to be alone with her so he could probe her deeper. The double entendre brought a grim smile.

Veering away from her, he stalked out of the kitchen.

The case he'd asked his personal butler to fetch was standing by the sofa in the living room. She spotted it the same time he did.

'You had my things removed from my room?' The incredulity in her voice amused and irritated him at once.

'I don't believe in wasting time when my mind is made up.'

'And what about *my* mind? You didn't know what choice I would make!'

'That's where you're wrong. I did. I'm very familiar with the concept of supply and demand. You want something only I can provide. You wanted it enough to hop on a plane on the strength of an eavesdropped conversation between complete strangers. I wagered on you being ambitious enough to agree to my demands.'

'You make me sound so mercenary.'

'On the contrary. I like a woman who states what she wants upfront. Subterfuge and false coyness are traits I actively despise.'

'Somehow I don't believe that.'

'You think I like liars?'

Her gaze slid away. 'I didn't say that.'

He forced himself to turn away, resume his path towards his bathroom and another cold shower. *Maledizione!*

'As for your case, I had it brought here to avoid any awkwardness. Or would you rather have answered questions as to why you've been absent from your duties for the last several hours?'

She groaned. 'Oh, God! What will they think?'

'They'll think the obvious. But you're with me, so no one will question you about it.'

'I...I...'

'The words you're looking for are *thank you*. You can use the second bedroom suite to get ready. I have a brunch meeting in the Dragon Room in half an hour.'

'And you want me to come with you?'

'Of course. From here on in, you serve no one but me.' His words echoed in his head and his fists clenched.

For the second time in less than ten minutes another unwanted emotion sideswiped him. *Possessiveness.*

Just as he'd trained himself not to trust, he'd trained himself not to become attached. Possessiveness suggested an attachment to something...*someone.*

Narciso didn't *do* attachment. And yet—

'What happens after your meeting?'

He forced nonchalance into his voice. 'We return here to indulge in...whatever we please. Tomorrow when the lock down is lifted, we leave.'

CHAPTER SIX

THE REST OF the morning turned out to be a study in how the very rich and influential operated. Having grown up in relative wealth and seen the lengths to which people went to keep what they had, Ruby had imagined she knew how power and influence were wielded.

Watching Narciso Valentino command a room just by walking into it took her education to a whole different level. People's attitude transformed just by him entering their presence, despite his mask now being back firmly in place.

Although dressed more casually than he'd been last night, he exuded the same authority and attention as he moved from room to room, chatting with other well-heeled guests. The brief time he left her to attend his meeting, Ruby was left with a floundering feeling in her stomach that irritated and shocked her at the same time.

She was finishing her buttered brioche and café Americano when she sensed a gaze on her. Anticipating another of the speculative looks she'd been on the receiving end of since she came downstairs with Narciso, she stemmed her apprehension and raised her head.

The man who'd played against Narciso last night and won thirty million dollars was watching her with stormy grey eyes.

He moved forward and pulled out a chair. 'May I join you?' He sat down before she could stop him.

'Sure. It's a free country, I think.'

His smile didn't quite reach his eyes. He steepled his fingers together and stared at her. 'Where's my… Where's your companion?'

'At a meeting…' She paused and stared down at his wrist. 'I thought those smartwatches could tell you where each guest is. Why are you asking me?'

'Perhaps I just wanted a conversation opener.'

'Needing an opener would mean you have something specific to discuss with me. I don't see what that could be.' Her discomfort grew underneath that unwavering, hostile stare. She started to put her flatware down, thought better of it and hung on to the knife.

His gaze went to it and swung back to hers. 'You won't be needing that.'

'I'll be the judge of that. Now, can I help you with something?' As she'd thought last night, there was something vaguely familiar about him. But like every single guest present, his mask was back on and nothing of the rest of his features was enough to pinpoint where she might have seen him before, and she was not going to commit another faux pas by asking him his name.

'I merely came to offer you a warning. Stay away from The Warlock.'

'Considering you won over thirty million dollars from him last night, I'd have thought you'd be in a better frame of mind, perhaps even celebrating your huge windfall, not wasting your time casting aspersions on someone you defeated.'

'He thinks he has bested me but he'll soon learn the error of his ways.'

'Right. Okay…was that all?' she asked, but his eyes had taken on a faraway look, as if he were somewhere else entirely.

'He's been poison ever since…' His mouth tightened and his eyes grew colder. 'For as long as I've had to deal with him, he's been nothing but trouble. He was given his name for a reason.'

'The Warlock?'

His hand fluttered in a dismissive gesture. 'No, I meant his real name. Take my advice and remember that once he tells you who he really is.'

'I'm not supposed to know who he is, so what you're saying means less than nothing to me.'

'Or you could understand perfectly what I mean.' His upper lips twisted. 'Unless spreading your legs for him has robbed you of all common sense.'

The barb struck too close to home. 'How dare you?' She jerked back at the sheer hatred pouring from him. Ice-cold sensation drenched her veins at the same time as warm hands cupped her shoulders.

'Ruby?' Narciso clipped out her name. 'What's going on here?' The question was quite rhetorical because she was sure he'd caught part of the exchange.

Certainly, his flint-hard gaze and tense jaw made her think of her earlier assessment of just how dangerous an opponent he could be.

For whatever reason, the man sitting across from her spewing vitriol had wronged Narciso Valentino on a very deep level. The skin around his mouth was white and the hands curved over her shoulders were a little less than gentle.

Ruby carefully set her knife down and took a deep breath. 'Nothing. He was just leaving. Weren't you?'

The older man smiled and took his time to rise. His eyes locked on Narciso's and for a moment Ruby thought she understood the connection, then dismissed it. What she was imagining couldn't be possible.

Pure visceral hate existed between these two men. It coloured the air and crawled over her skin.

In her darkest days before she'd actively distanced herself from her parents, her father's behaviour had permeated every single corner of her existence and she'd imagined she hated him. She could never accept the way Ricardo Trevelli lived his life, or the careless way he treated her mother. But she'd never encountered hate this strong. It was a potent, living thing.

She shivered. Narciso felt it and glanced down at her before refocusing on her unwanted guest.

'Do I need to teach you another lesson, old man?'

'Keep your money, hotshot. I understand the need to brag in front of your woman. Shame it had to cost you so much last night.'

'It was worth it to see your face. If you need a refresher on how to win, I can accommodate you.'

The old man sneered. 'The time is coming when I'll wipe that smug look off your face once and for all.'

Narciso's smile was arctic. 'Do it quickly, then. I'm growing tired of your empty promises.'

Ruby sucked in a shocked breath at the blatant taunt. With a thick swear word that would singe the ears off a Sicilian donkey, the old man swivelled on his heel and walked away.

Narciso pulled back her chair, caught her up and swung her around to face him. 'What did he say to you?' he demanded, his nostrils pinched hard with the anger he was holding back.

'Oh, he was educating me on the real meaning of your name, albeit very cryptically. Who is he anyway?'

He looked after the departing man and visibly inhaled.

'I told you—he's no one important. But I want you to stay away from him.'

'That would be difficult since I don't even know who he is.'

Tucking her arm through the crook of his elbow, he led her out of the dining area styled with large, exquisitely scrolled Chinese screens. She'd heard one of the guests comment that the stands holding up the scrolls were made of solid gold. *Q Virtus,* its mysterious owner, Zeus…in fact this whole place was insane with its surrealistic extravagance, secrecy and decadence.

'You're an intelligent woman, hopefully equipped with enough of that intuition you women are so proud of. Use it and stay clear of him.'

'Funny, he said the same thing about you. And why does that sound suspiciously like a threat?'

He led her into another express lift and used his thumbprint and her smartwatch to activate the panel before pressing the button for the sub-basement.

'Because it is one.'

'So we've graduated from ropes to threats?' Her attempt at humour fell flat when his face tightened further.

'Don't tempt me. I'm this close to breaking point.' He held two fingers together for emphasis.

She froze when the arm imprisoning hers drew her closer to his warm body. 'Did something go wrong with your meeting? A deal fall through or something?'

'What makes you ask that?'

'Aside from the confrontation just now, you seem to be in a foul mood. Did something happen?'

'No, sweet Ruby. The "network hard" part of my day is ticking along nicely. It's the "play harder" part that has failed miserably.'

So she was partly to blame for his disagreeable mood.

Time for a subject change.

'Where to now?'

'The champagne mixer in the Blue Dungeon. Then we're leaving,' he clipped out.

'I thought we couldn't leave until the lock down was lifted tonight?'

'I've asked for a special dispensation from Zeus,' he said, his gaze on the downward-moving arrow. They were sinking deeper into the bowels of the building. Ruby felt as if she were disappearing into Alice's Wonderland. 'The dispensation should be coming through on your smartwatch any minute now. Let me know when it does.'

'The owner's name really *is* Zeus. Seriously?'

'You don't find my moniker incredulous.'

'That's because…' She paused, unwilling to voice the thought rattling through her head.

'Because?'

She shrugged. 'The Warlock suits you, somehow.'

He faced her fully, his gaze raking her face in that intensely raw way that made her feel vulnerable, exposed.

'In what way does it suit me?' he asked silkily.

Because you mesmerise me with very little effort. Ruby cleared her throat.

'You're obviously a genius at what you do.'

'And you think my success stems from sorcery?'

She shrugged. 'Not in the chicken bones and goat sacrificing sense but in other ways.'

One hand rose, trailed down her jaw to rest on the pulse pounding at her throat. 'And will I be able to sway you into my bed with this potent magic of mine?'

'No.'

His smile this time was genuine. And devastating to her senses. 'You sound so very sure.'

'Because I am. I told you, I don't mix business and pleasure.'

His smile dimmed. 'Would this have anything to do with your ex-almost-lover?'

'I believe it's a sound work ethic,' she answered.

Once Narciso had left her on her own, she'd replayed the events of last night and this morning. Shame at her behaviour had charged through her, forcing her to quickly reinforce her crumbling self-control.

Letting her feelings run wild and free was not an option. Heartache and devastation could be the only result if she didn't get herself back under control.

'So you intend to let him win?' Narciso queried softly.

'This is *my* choice.'

'If you say so.'

She had no chance to respond before the doors opened and they entered the most surreal room Ruby had ever seen. Blue lights had been placed strategically on the floors, walls and ceilings of a huge cavern. And bottles of champagne hung on wires, their labels combined with the words *QV Macau.*

'What does *Q Virtus* mean?' she asked.

His smile was mysterious. 'I could tell you but I'd have to—'

'Oh, never mind.' She turned as an excited murmur went through the crowd.

Six acrobats clad in LED-lit costumes swung from tension cables from one end of the room to the other.

She couldn't help her gasp of wonder at their movement. 'Oh, my God.'

'So *that's* what it'll sound like.' The wicked rasp was for her ears alone. His warm breath tickled her ear, sending a tingle right to her toes.

'What *what* will sound like?'

'Your gasp of wonder when I'm deep inside you.' His lips touched her lobe and she jerked at the electric sensation.

'Since that's never going to happen, you'll just have to keep guessing,' she replied.

He merely laughed and plucked two glasses off a sterling-silver tray that dropped down from the ceiling as if by magic. 'Champagne?' He passed her a glass.

She took it simply for something to do besides staring at his gorgeous face, which had transformed dramatically from his earlier formidable demeanour. He clinked glasses with her and raised his in a toast. 'To the thrill of the challenge.'

'I won't participate.'

'Too late. You threw the gauntlet. I accepted. Drink your champagne. That's a five-thousand-dollar glass you're holding.'

She stared down into the golden liquid before answering. 'I don't really drink that much.'

'I guessed as much. Another souvenir from the ex?'

The pain of the memory scythed through her before she could guard herself against it. She shook her head.

'Why don't you drink, Ruby?' His voice was hypnotic, pulling on a cord deep inside that made her want to reveal everything to him.

'I don't like the loss of control it gives me.'

Silver eyes narrowed. 'Something happened to you?'

'You could say that.'

'Something bad?'

'Depends on your definition of bad. Someone upset me. I thought getting drunk would solve the problem. It didn't. It made it worse.'

'Who was it?'

'My father—' She stopped as she realised how much she was revealing to him.

'Ah, *sì*. Fathers. It's such a shame they're necessary for evolution, isn't it?' Although his words were light, his eyes had taken on that haunted look she'd glimpsed this morning in his kitchen.

Out of nowhere came the overwhelming urge to take his pain away. 'I can't believe we're standing in one of the most spectacular rooms I've ever seen, discussing our daddy issues.'

'You're discussing *your* daddy issues. I have none.'

She frowned. 'But you just said—'

His mouth tightened 'I merely expressed a view on evolution.' He took a large slug of his drink and set the glass aside. 'Come, the show's about to begin.'

He walked her deeper into the room, to an even larger space where a stage was brightly lit in hues of blue and green.

Several more acrobats struck different poses from their ropes but as the oriental-themed music filled the room they started to perform as one. Immediately she recognised the world-renowned group whose exclusivity was reserved to royalty and the crème de la crème of A-listers.

The fluidity of their movement and sheer talent taken to hone such an awe-inspiring performance kept Ruby mesmerised for several minutes, until she noticed Narciso's renewed tension. A glimpse at his profile showed a tense jaw and tightly pursed lips.

She debated for a second, then took a breath.

'It's okay if you don't want to admit to having daddy issues. I lived in denial myself for a long time,' she whispered, aware several guests stood close by.

'Excuse me?' he rasped.

'I could apologise but I thought we were…you know…sharing.'

'I don't *share,* Ruby. At least not in that way.'

'Listen—'

'You're missing the show,' he cut across her.

Forced to curb her reply, she resumed watching the show, aware that he grew tenser with every passing minute.

A particularly daring acrobat surged right over their heads. Narciso's hand tightened around hers. Thinking he was reacting to the spectacular display, she glanced at him, to find his gaze fixed across the stage, on the man who'd confronted her less than an hour ago.

In that instant, the resemblance between them struck her hard. Their similar heights, their silver eyes, the proud, arrogant way they viewed the world. How could she not have seen it until now?

'Oh, my God, he's your father.'

He stiffened and glanced down at her with cold, grim eyes. 'He's a man whose DNA I happen to share. Nothing more.'

Applause broke through the crowd as the show finished in a crescendo of dives and leaps choreographed so fabulously, she couldn't help but clap despite her shocking discovery.

They were father and son. And they hated each other with a passion that was almost a separate being every time they were within feet of each other.

She wanted to know what had placed such a wide divide between them but she held her tongue. She had no right to pry into anyone's life. Her own baggage was enough to be dealing with. After fighting for so long and so hard to get away from the noxious environment her parents chose to inhabit, the last thing she wanted was for someone like Narciso Valentino to dredge it all up.

The smartwatch on her wrist beeped twice.

Narciso glanced down at it. 'We're leaving.'

Her heart climbed into her throat, and she fought the snap of excitement fizzing through her. What on earth was wrong with her? She couldn't be secretly thrilled with the thought of being alone with this man.

Could she?

Within minutes their cases were being loaded into the trunk of the stretch limo that stood idling in the underground car park, with a smartly dressed driver poised at the door. She slid in and Narciso joined her.

The moment the door shut, she wanted to fling it open and dive out. She'd thought she was venturing into the unknown by coming to Macau.

By agreeing to go to Belize with The Warlock of Wall Street, she was really stepping into an abyss.

'I…don't think I can…' She stopped. What was she doing? She'd forced herself to endure a TV show after Simon had convinced her it was the only way she could fund Dolce Italia.

She'd plunged herself into the very environment she'd grown up in and actively detested just so she could establish her independence. Now she stood on the threshold of seeing it pay off.

'Having second thoughts?' he asked as the car rolled up a ramp and exited into bright mid-afternoon sunshine.

'No. I'm not,' she insisted more to herself than to him.

'Good.'

The smartwatch emitted several discreet beeps. 'What's it doing?'

'It's erasing the evidence of my activities here.'

'Wow, you're not part of the CIA, are you?'

'I could be if spies are your thing.' He gave another of those wicked smiles and her mouth dried.

'I'll pass, thanks. Although I'm curious what you have to do to belong to a club like that.' She took the watch off and examined its multifaceted detail.

'It involves a lot more than chicken bones and goat sacrifices, I can assure you.'

Against her will, a smile tugged at her mouth. Letting go, she laughed. He joined her, his perfectly even teeth flashing in the sunlight. The deep sound echoed in the enclosed space and wrapped itself around her.

Danger! Her senses screamed again. But it was a seductive

danger, akin to knowing that extra mouthful of rich, decadent mousse was deadly for you but being unable to resist the taste.

And she'd quickly discovered that if she let herself fall under his spell, he would completely bypass her hips and go straight to her heart.

'Here, take this back.' She held out his watch, stressing to herself that she didn't miss having something of his so close to her skin.

'Keep it. It's yours.'

'Are you serious?' she gasped. 'But what about its value—'

'I wasn't thinking of its monetary value when I offered it. And if you're thinking about pawning it, think twice.'

'I meant its sentimental value to you, of your visit here? And I'd never pawn a gift!'

'I'm happy to hear it. As for sentiments, I prefer mine to be warm-blooded.' He took off his mask and laid it on his knee. 'Luckily, I have you.'

The statement sent equal parts of apprehension and excitement through her. She slowly slid the watch back onto her wrist, and watched as they approached the Pearl River. Luxury super yachts in all shapes and sizes lined the marina.

The limo drew to a stop beside a sleek speedboat and Narciso helped her out. The driver held out a leather case, its velvet inside carved in the exact shape of his mask. Narciso placed the mask inside, shut the case and handed it to the driver.

Seconds after their luggage was loaded, the pilot guided the boat towards the open river.

'I've spent a lot of time asking you where we're going but I need to ask you one more time.'

'Don't you trust me?' he asked with a mockingly raised brow. 'No.'

He laughed again. And again, the sound tugged deep inside.

'We're heading to the airport. My private jet will fly us to Belize.'

Nodding, she watched the disappearing skyline of Macau City. It'd earned its name, Vegas of the East, but there was also soul in this place, and in other circumstances Ruby would've loved to explore a lot more.

She turned to find him watching her. The hunger was back in his eyes, coupled with a dangerous restlessness.

'What?' she demanded when she couldn't stand his intense scrutiny any longer.

'I came here for a purpose. You succeeded in swaying me from that purpose. I intend to find out why.'

'Was that purpose to destroy your father?' she asked before she thought better of it.

He immediately stiffened. The breeze rushing over the water ruffled his hair. He slowly scythed his fingers through it without taking his eyes off her.

'Among other things.'

'But you decided to spare him at the last minute.'

'A very puzzling notion indeed.'

Her heart hammered as his speculative gaze rested on her lips.

'I don't think it's puzzling at all. I think you knew exactly what you were doing.'

His eyes narrowed. 'And what would that be, O Wise One?'

'You were extending the thrill of the chase, delaying the gratification of the kill blow.'

'How very astute of you.'

'So what were the other things?'

'Perdono?'

'You said among other things.'

His gaze drifted down the neckline of her black tube dress, again a tighter fit than she would've preferred. 'What do you think?'

'According to online sources you have an IQ of a hundred and forty-eight.'

'It's closer to one-fifty but who's counting?'

Her mouth pursed. 'It also says you're a rampantly rabid playboy who thinks about nothing else but the next woman he intends to sleep with. It's a shame you've chosen to use *all* hundred and fifty to chase skirts.'

He grinned. 'No, I only use one hundred and forty-eight. I need the other two to walk and talk.'

She rolled her eyes even though the corners of her mouth curved. The boat pulled up to a jetty, beyond which she could see several planes parked on tarmac.

Narciso's plane was the same silver shade as his eyes, with a black trim that made it stand out among the other jets.

He lived a life of extreme luxury and decadence, while making people like her jump through hoops to claim what was rightfully theirs.

'What's wrong? You're frowning.'

'You're asking me to spend time and energy claiming something that should be already mine. I'm trying to see the fairness in that.'

'Something about going the extra mile? Doing whatever it takes?' he mocked, but his eyes held a flash of warning. 'Get on the plane, Ruby.'

'Or what?'

'Or you lose everything. Because I won't renegotiate and I despise being thwarted.'

Her feet remained leaden. Her instinct warned her she wouldn't emerge unscathed if she went with him.

'Is this how you do business? You strike a deal, you renegotiate, then you renege?' he demanded.

'Of course not. I'm only here because *your* company reneged on the deal it struck with me!'

'A fact I'm yet to verify. The quicker you get on the plane, the quicker this can be resolved.'

She had no argument against that. And the reality was she'd come too far to turn back. And there was the small problem of Simon's loan shark lurking in the background.

Taking a deep breath, she started to mount the steps. Recalling something he'd said, she twisted and nearly collided with his lean, muscular frame. The steadying hand he threw around her waist burned through to her skin. This close, without the hindrance of his mask, she could see how his envy-inducing cheekbones and long eyelashes framed his impossibly handsome face.

'What did you mean about being thwarted?'

'Sex, Ruby. I meant sex. We're going to have it together. It's going to be spectacular and, yes, I know you're going to protest. But it will happen. So prepare yourself for it.'

She was still reeling from the raw, brazen words hours later as she tried to doze in her fully reclined seat two rows from where he conducted a teleconference call.

She had no idea how long the flight to Belize would take. She had no idea what the temperature would be this time of year.

In fact, her mind was empty of everything but the words Narciso had uttered to her on the steps of his plane.

Punching her pillow, she silently cursed herself for dwelling on it. It was *never* going to happen. She'd have to be ten kinds of fool to repeat what she'd nearly gone through with Simon—

'If you punch that pillow one more time, it'll give up its secrets, I'm sure of it.'

She twisted around and found him standing beside her seat, one hand held out.

'Sleep is eluding you. Let's spend some time together.'

'No, thanks.'

He dropped his hand and shoved it into his pocket. Ruby tried not to stare at the way his shoulders flexed under the snow-white T-shirt he'd changed into. 'Please yourself. But if you end up serving me food that I find abhorrent because you haven't done your homework, you'll only have yourself to blame.'

The challenge had the desired effect. Pushing aside the cashmere throw the stewardess had provided, she went after him.

He smiled mockingly and waved her into the club chair opposite his.

Ruby smoothed her dishevelled hair down, and activated her tablet. 'Okay, shoot. What's your favourite food?'

'Life offers such vast richness. Having favourites is severely restricting.'

She sighed. 'This isn't going to be easy, is it?'

He shrugged. 'I take entertainment where I can get it.'

'Okay, next question. Any food allergies?'

'Peanuts and avocado.'

Her head snapped up. 'Seriously?'

'I don't joke with my health, *amante*.'

She noted it on her tablet. 'How do you feel about Sicilian food?'

'I'm completely indifferent.'

She looked up in surprise. 'Really? Most Sicilians are passionate about everything to do with their homeland.'

'Probably because they have a connection to be passionate about—' He stopped suddenly and his jaw clenched.

She watched him try to rein in his control and her chest tightened. 'And you don't?'

Tension gripped his frame. 'Not for a long time.'

Her tablet dimmed, but she didn't reactivate it. The flash of anguish in his eyes snagged her attention.

'Because of your father?' she pushed.

His eyes narrowed. 'Why does this interest you so much?'

The question took her aback, made her ask herself the same thing. 'I...I thought we were making conversation.'

'This is one subject I prefer to steer clear of. *Capisce?*'

'Because you find it upsetting.'

He cursed under his breath and raked back his hair as that stubborn lock fell over his forehead again. 'Not at all. The subject of my father fires up my blood. I just prefer not to discuss it with near strangers.'

Despite cautioning herself to stick to business, she found herself replying, 'Haven't you heard of the saying make love not war?'

'Why do I need to choose one when I can have both? I'll make love to you and I make war with Giacomo.'

'For how long?'

'How long can I make love to you? Is that another challenge to my manhood?'

'I meant your father, and you know it.'

'I intend to keep going until one of us is in the ground.'

She gasped. 'You don't really mean that, do you?'

Again that flash of pain, gone before it'd even formed. '*Si*, I do.'

'You know, he called you poison.'

This time the anguish stayed for several seconds, shattered his expression. Her heart fractured at the pain she glimpsed before his face settled into neutral indifference. 'He's right. I am poison.'

His unflinching admission made her heart contract. 'What happened between you two?'

'I was born.'

Narciso watched her try to make sense of his reply. She frowned, then shook her head. 'I don't understand.'

He wanted to laugh but the vice gripping his chest every time he thought of Giacomo made that impossible. He rose and walked to the bar at the mid-section of his plane. Pouring two glasses of mineral water, he brought one to her and gulped down the other. 'That's because you're trying to decipher a hidden meaning. There is none. I was born. And Giacomo has hated that reality ever since.'

'He hates being a father?'

He paused before answering, unwilling to utter the words he hadn't said aloud for a very long time, not since he'd wailed it as a pathetic little boy to the housekeeper who'd been the closest thing he'd known to a mother.

'No. He hates me.'

Shock darkened Ruby's eyes.

He sat back down abruptly, and willed back the control he'd

felt slipping from him since he'd walked into the poker den in Macau last night. He glanced up and saw sympathy blazing from Ruby's face. The rawness abated a little but, no matter how much he tried, he couldn't shake off the unsettling emptiness inside him.

He swallowed his water and set the glass down.

'Enough about me. Tell me about *your* father.'

She stiffened. 'I'd rather not.'

'You were ready to *share* just a little while ago.' He settled deeper into his seat and watched her face. And it was a stunning face. The combination of innocence and defiance in her eyes kept him intrigued. She didn't hide her emotions very well. Right now, she was fighting pain and squirming with a desire to change the subject.

The sudden urge to help her, to offer the same sympathy she'd just exhibited, took him by surprise.

Dio, what was wrong with him?

This woman who'd flown thousands of miles after him was an enigma. An enigma with daddy issues. He should be staying well clear.

He leaned forward. 'Since you seem shocked by the depth of my...feelings towards Giacomo, I'm assuming your feelings towards your father are much less...volatile?'

Those full lips he wanted to taste again so badly pressed together for a moment. 'I don't hate my father, no. But I prefer to keep my distance from them.'

'*Them?*'

She fidgeted. 'You're going to find out anyway. My parents are Ricardo and Paloma Trevelli.'

Her stare held a little defiance and a whole load of vulnerability. 'Sorry, you lost me.'

A delicate frown marred her perfect skin. Again his fingers ached to touch. Soon, he promised himself.

'How come you own several media companies and yet have no clue what goes on in the world?'

'My line of work doesn't mean I compromise my privacy. So your parents are famous?'

Her eyelids swept down to cover her expression. 'You could say that. They're famous celebrity TV chefs.'

'And their fame disgusts you?' he deduced.

Blue eyes flicked to his. 'I didn't say that.'

'Your voice. Your eyes. Your body. They all give you away, Ruby Trevelli.' He loved the way her name sounded on his lips. He wanted to keep saying it... 'So you despise them for being famous and cashing in on it. Isn't that what you're doing?'

'No! I'd never whore myself the way—' She stopped and bit her lip.

'Do they know you have this view of them?' he asked.

She shrugged. 'They've chosen a lifestyle I prefer not to be a part of. It's that simple.'

'Ruby...' he waited until her eyes met his '...we both know it's not that simple.'

Shadows chased across her face and her mouth trembled before she firmed it again. Before he could think twice, he reached out and touched her hand.

She swallowed hard, then pulled her tablet towards her. 'How many people will I be catering for at your event?'

He told himself he wasn't disappointed by her withdrawal. 'Are we back to all business again?'

'Yes. I think it's safer, don't you?'

Narciso couldn't deny the veracity of that. Dredging up his past was the last thing he'd intended when he'd boarded his plane. And yet, he resented her switch to all-business mode.

'If you say so,' he replied. 'You think you can handle a VIP dinner?'

'I believe in my talent as much as you believe in your abilities as the Warlock of Wall Street. If I say I'll rock your socks off, I will.'

A reluctant smile tugged at his lips. 'A confident woman is such a turn-on.'

She glared at him. 'If you say so,' she replied sweetly. 'Is there a guest of honour that I should pay particular attention to?'

'Vladimir Rudenko. I'm in the last stages of ironing out a deal with him. He's the VIP guest.'

She started to make another note when her tablet pinged. He heard her sharp intake of breath before she paled.

'What is it?'

'It's nothing.'

The blatant lie set his teeth on edge. 'Don't lie to me.' He reached for the tablet but she snatched it off the table.

'It's a private thing, all right?'

'A private thing that's obviously upset you.' He watched her chest rise and fall in agitation and experienced that disconcerting urge to help again.

'Yes, but it's my problem and I'll deal with it.'

Before he could probe further, she jumped up. 'You said I could use the bedroom if I wanted. I'll go finish making my notes now and get some sleep, if that's okay?'

It wasn't okay with him. Nothing had been okay since he met Ruby Trevelli. But short of physically restraining her, an action sure to bring brimstone upon his head, he let her go.

'We won't be landing for another six hours. I'll wake you before we do.'

She nodded quickly. 'Thanks.'

He watched her walk away, her short, tight black dress framing her body so deliciously, his groin hardened. He couldn't suppress his frustrated growl as the bedroom door shut after her.

The image of her lying in his bed haunted him. But those images were soon replaced by other, more disturbing ones as his thoughts turned to their earlier conversation.

His father.

He shoved a hand through his hair. He'd come so close to revealing the old, bottled-up pain. Hell, he'd even contemplated spilling his guts about Maria.

Maria. The tool his father had used to hammer home how much he detested his son.

His laptop beeped with an incoming message. Casting another glance at the bedroom door, Narciso pursed his lips.

The next six hours would be devoted to clearing his schedule.

Because once they were in Belize, he would devote his time to deciphering the code that was Ruby Trevelli and why she had succeeded in getting under his skin.

CHAPTER SEVEN

SHE WAS WARM. And comfortable. The steady sound drumming in her ears soothed her, made her feel safe from the erratic dreams that still played in her mind.

But she wanted to get warmer still. Wanted to burrow in the solid strength surrounding her.

The heart beating underneath her cheek—

Ruby jerked awake.

'Easy now, tigress. You'll do yourself an injury.'

'What the hell…? What are you doing here?'

'Sharing the bed. As you can see, once again I managed to restrain myself. And this time we're both fully clothed. That means I win brownie points.'

'You win nothing for letting yourself into my bed uninvited.'

'Technically, this is my bed, Goldilocks. Besides, you were muttering in your sleep and tossing and turning when I looked in on you. I had to make sure you didn't sleepwalk yourself out of an emergency exit in your agitation.'

Ruby tried to pry herself away from the inviting length of his warm body, but the arm clamped around her waist refused to move. 'I wasn't that agitated.'

Silver eyes pinned hers. 'Yes, you were. Tell me what upset you.' His voice was cajoling, hypnotic.

She wanted to tell him about the undeniable threat in the email that had made a shaft of ice pierce her nape and shimmer down her spine. The loan shark had stepped up his threat level, implicating her mother.

Ironic that Narciso, the world-famous playboy and media mogul, had no idea who her mother was but some two-bit loan shark who inhabited the dregs of society knew who Paloma Trevelli was enough to threaten to break her legs if Ruby didn't reply with a timescale of payment.

Her reply had bought her a few more days but there was no way she intended to tell Narciso what was going on.

'I told you. It's my business to handle.'

'Not if it will potentially impede your ability to perform your job.'

'I can cook blindfolded.'

'That I would pay good money to see.' He pulled her closer, wedging his thigh more firmly between hers so she was trapped. Some time during sleep, she'd curled her hand over his chest. Now, firm muscles transmitted heat to her fingers, making them tingle.

Awareness jolted through her when his lips drifted up her cheek to her temple. 'If we weren't landing in less than thirty minutes, I'd take this a step further, use other means to find out what's going on.'

'You're operating under the assumption that I would've permitted it.'

He laughed, then sobered. 'It wasn't your father, was it?'

'No, it wasn't.'

He stared down at her for a long time, then nodded. 'I did some research while you were asleep. I know about your parents.'

'Oh?' She couldn't help the wave of anxiety that washed over her.

His eyes narrowed. 'Has it always been like that with them?'

That mingled thread of pain and humiliation when she thought of them tightened like a vice around her heart. 'You mean the crazy circus?'

He nodded.

'Until I went to college, yes. I didn't return home afterward. And I have minimal contact these days. Any more and it gets… unpleasant.'

'For whom?'

'For everyone. My father is a serial adulterer who doesn't understand why I won't condone his behaviour. My mother doesn't understand why I don't forgive my father every time he strays. They both want me to join the family business. The same business for which they shamelessly exploit their fame, their family, their friends—' She ground to a halt and tried to breathe around the pain in her chest.

His hand stroked down her cheek. 'You hate yourself for the way you feel.'

Feeling exposed, she tried to pull away. He held her firmer. 'Ruby *mio,* I think you'll agree we went way past business when we spent the night together in my bed. Talk to me,' he coaxed.

She drew in a shaky breath and reassured herself that they were talking. Just talking. 'I hate that my family is broken and I can't see a way to fix it without being forced to live my life in a media circus.'

'And yet you chose that avenue to fund your business.'

'Believe me, it wasn't my first choice.'

'Then why did you do it?'

'We'd tried getting loans from the banks with no success. Simon heard about the show and convinced me to enter. Taking three weeks out of my life to be on the show felt like a worthy sacrifice.'

'So you returned to the thing you hate the most in order to achieve your goal.'

'Does that make me a fool?'

'No, it makes you brave.'

The unexpected compliment made her heart stutter. Silver eyes rested on her, assessing her so thoroughly, she squirmed. Of course the movement made her body rub dangerously against his.

He emitted a leonine growl and the arm around her waist

tightened. One hand caught her bent leg and hitched it higher between his legs. The bold imprint of his erection seared her thigh. Heat flared between them, raw and fervent.

'So you don't think it's wrong to do whatever it takes to achieve one's dreams?'

His eyes darkened. 'No. In fact, it's a trait I wholeheartedly admire.'

Her throat clogged at the sincerity in his voice. The barriers she'd tried so hard to shore up threatened to crumble again. A pithy, mocking Narciso was bad enough. A gentle, caring Narciso in whose eyes she saw nothing but admiration and praise was even more dangerous to her already fragile emotions.

Scrambling to regroup, she laughed. 'Dear God, am I dreaming? That's two compliments within—'

'Enough,' he snapped. Then he kissed her.

Ruby's heart soared at the ferocity of his kiss. Desire swept over her, burying the volatile memories under even more turbulent currents of passion as he mercilessly explored her mouth with a skill that left her reeling.

Narciso could kiss. She already had proof of that. But this time the sharper edge of hunger added another dimension that made her heart pump frantically, as she saw no let-up in the erotic torrents buffeting her.

When he sank back against the pillows and pulled her on top of him, she went willingly. Strong, demanding hands slid up her bare thighs to cup her bottom, press her against that solid evidence of his need.

Unfamiliar hunger shot through her belly to arrow between her legs. Desperate to ease it, she rocked her hips deeper into him.

His thick groan echoed between their fused lips. He surged up to meet her, thrusting against her in an undeniable move that made her blood pound harder.

With her damp centre plastered so firmly and fully against him, she moaned as the beginnings of a tingle seized her spine. Hunger tore through her as rough fingers bit into her hips, keeping her firmly in place as they found a superb synchronicity that needed no words.

The first wave of sensation hit her from nowhere. She cried out, her fingers spiking into his hair as she grasped stability in a world gone haywire.

'*Dio!* Let go, baby. Let go.'

The hot words, crooned in her ear from a voice she'd found mesmerising from the very first, were the final catalyst. With a jagged moan, Ruby gave into the bliss smashing through her. She melted on top of him, giving in to the hands petting down her back as her shudders eased.

'I don't know whether to celebrate for making you come while we're both fully dressed or spank you for your appalling timing.'

Slowly, the realisation of what she'd just done pierced her euphoria.

Beneath her cheek, his heart raced. She could feel his erection still raging, strong and vital.

She'd orgasmed on top of Narciso Valentino and he hadn't even needed to undress her.

'*Oh, God.*'

Narciso held himself very still. He had to, or risk tearing her clothes off and taking her with the force of a rutting bull.

'God isn't going to help you now, naughty Ruby. You have to deal with me.'

'I... That shouldn't have happened.'

He nodded grimly. 'I agree.'

Wide blue eyes locked on his. 'You do?'

He swallowed hard. 'It should've happened when I was inside you. Now I feel woefully deprived.' Unable to stop himself, he moved his hands up and down her back. He tensed as her breathing changed. Desire thickened the air once more. Sensing her about to bolt, he flipped her over and trapped her underneath him. 'But I have you now.'

She tried to wriggle away but all she did was exacerbate the flashflood of desire drowning them both.

'No, I can't… We can't do this.'

He stiffened. 'Why not?'

'It won't end well. Simon—'

His eyes narrowed into warning slits. 'Was a cheating low-life who didn't deserve you. You and I together…we're different. We deserve each other.'

Narciso speared his fingers into her soft hair. But instead of kissing her, he grazed his lips along her jaw and down her throat to the pulse racing crazily there. He drew down her sleeves, exposing her breasts to his mouth. His mind screamed at him to stop before it was too late, but he was already sliding his tongue over one nipple.

Dio! He'd never known a woman to smash so effortlessly through his defences.

Her nails raked his nape and he groaned in approval. By the time he turned his attention to her other nipple, her whimpers were adding fire to his raging arousal.

She tugged on his shirt and he gave in to her demand. With a ragged laugh, he helped her reef it over his head and divested her of her dress.

Stark hunger consumed him as he took a moment to feast his eyes on her exposed body. 'You're so beautiful.' He drifted a hand down her chest and over her stomach to the top of her panties.

That disconcerting throb of possessiveness rocked through him again. He didn't want to know who else she'd been with but, in that moment, Narciso was glad her ex-business partner had failed to make her his. He settled himself over her, taking her mouth in a scorching kiss that obliterated words and feelings he didn't want to examine too closely.

His hand slid over her panties, hungrily seeking the heart of her. Her breath caught as his fingers breached her dampness and flicked over her sensitive flesh.

She jerked and squeezed her eyes tightly shut.

'Open your eyes, *amante*,' he commanded. He wanted…no, *needed* to see her, to assure himself that she was sliding into insanity just as quickly as he was. When she refused to comply, he applied more pressure. 'Do it or I'll stop.'

Eyes full of arousal slowly opened. His breath fractured at the electrifying connection. His whole body tightened to breaking point and he mentally shook his head.

What the hell was happening here?

Her delicate shudder slowed his flailing thoughts. Absorbing her reaction, he inserted one finger inside her, drinking in her hitched cry as she shuddered again.

'*Dio,* you're so tight.' He waited until she'd adjusted, then pressed in another finger.

Narciso was unprepared for her wince.

Instantly alert, he asked, 'What's wrong?'

She shook her head but he could see the trepidation in her eyes.

Those now familiar alarm bells shrieked. 'Answer me, Ruby.'

Nervously, she licked her lips. 'I'm…a virgin.'

Shock doused him in ice. For several seconds he couldn't move. Then the realisation of how close he'd come to taking her, to staking a claim on what he had no right to, hit him like a ton of bricks.

He surged back from her, reefing a hand through his hair as he inhaled sharply.

'You're a virgin,' he repeated numbly.

Raising her chin, she stared back at him. 'Yes.'

Several puzzle pieces finally slotted into place—the touches of innocence he'd spotted, her bolshiness even as she seemed out of her depth.

Her trepidation.

What had he said a moment ago—they *deserved* each other? Not any more.

Regret bit deep as he forced himself off the bed. 'Then, *cara mia,* this is over.'

Ruby came out of the bathroom of her cabin and slowed to a stop. Glancing around her room, she tried again to grapple with the sheer opulence around her. The three-decked yacht, complete with helicopter landing pad, had made her jaw drop the first time she'd seen it two days ago.

But the inside of Narciso's yacht was even more luxurious.

Black with a silver trim on the outside, it was an exact reverse on the inside. Silver and platinum vied with Carrara marble mined from the exclusive quarries north of Tuscany.

Her suite, complete with queen-size bed, sunken Jacuzzi bath and expensive toiletries, was the last word in luxury.

But all the opulence couldn't stem the curious emptiness inside her.

Since her arrival in Belize, she'd barely seen Narciso. The only times she saw him was when she served the list of meals he'd approved the day they'd boarded *The Warlock*.

At first the studied consideration with which he'd treated her after she'd blurted her confession had surprised her. Who knew he was the sort of playboy who treated virgins as if they were sacred treasures?

But then she'd seen the look in his eyes. The regret. The banked pain. Her surprise had morphed into confusion.

She was still confused now as she tugged off her towel and headed for the drawer that held her meagre clothes. Only to stop dead at the sight of the monogrammed leather suitcase standing at the bottom of the bed.

She opened it. Silk sarongs, bikinis, sundresses, designer shoes and slippers fell out of the case as she dug through it, her stomach hollowing out with incredulity.

Dressing in the jeans and top she'd travelled to Macau in and taken to wearing since her arrival simply because the three evening gowns were totally out of the question, she went in search of the elusive Sicilian who seemed hell-bent on keeping her permanently off balance.

She found him on the middle deck, after getting lost twice. He wore white linen shorts and a dark blue polo shirt. The early evening sun slanted over jet-black hair, highlighting its vibrancy and making her recall how it had felt to run her hands through the strands.

The sight of his bare legs made her swallow before she reminded herself she wasn't going to be affected by his stunning physique any longer. He'd pointedly avoided her for two whole days. She was damned if she'd let him catch her drinking him in as if he were her last hope for sustenance.

She was here to do a job. Whatever closeness they'd shared on his plane was gone, a temporary aberration never to be repeated. Her focus now needed to be on what she'd come here to do. But before that...

'You bought me clothes?' she asked.

He turned around, casually shoving his hands into his pockets. When his eyes met hers, she couldn't read a single expression in the silver depths. The Narciso who'd alternately laughed, mocked and devoured her with his eyes was gone. In his place was a coolly remote stranger.

'The size of your suitcase suggested you'd packed for a short stay. This is a solution to a potential problem. Unless you plan on wearing those jeans every day for the next week?'

True, in the strong Belizean sun, they felt hot and sticky on her skin. Not to mention they were totally inappropriate for the job she was here to do. When she cooked, she preferred looser, comfortable clothes.

But still. 'I could've sorted my own wardrobe.'

'You're here on my schedule. Making time for you to go shopping doesn't feature on there.'

'I wouldn't have—'

'It was no big deal, Ruby. Let's move on. It's time to step up your game. I want to see how you fare with a three-course meal. Michel will assist you if you need it.' He glanced at his watch. 'I'd like to eat at seven, which gives you two hours.'

The arrogant dismissal made her hackles rise. The distance between them made her feel on edge, bereft.

She assured herself it was better this way. But deep down, an ache took root.

Michel, Narciso's chef, greeted her with an openly friendly smile when she entered the kitchen.

'What do you have in mind for today for *monsieur?*' the Frenchman asked. Deep blue eyes remained contemplative as he stared at her.

'He wants to eat at seven so I was thinking of making a special bruschetta to start and chicken parmigiana main if we have the ingredients?'

'Of course. I bought fresh supplies this morning from town.'

The mention of town made her wonder when Narciso had bought her clothes. Had he shopped for them himself or given instructions?

Shaking her head to dispel the useless wondering, she followed Michel into the pantry. 'Oh...heaven!' She fell on the plump tomatoes and aubergines and squealed when she saw the large heads of truffles carefully packed in a box.

Freshly sliced prosciutto hung from specially lined containers that kept it from drying out and Parma ham stayed cool in a nearby chiller.

Michel took out the deboned chicken breast in the fridge. 'Would you like me to cut it up for you?'

'Normally, I'd say yes, but I think it's best if I do everything myself.' She smiled to take the sting out of the refusal.

He shrugged. 'Shout if you need anything.' After helping himself to a bottle of water, he left her alone.

Ruby selected the best knife and began chopping garlic, onions and the fresh herbs Michel kept in the special potted containers in the pantry.

The sense of calm and pure joy in bringing the ingredients together finally soothed the unsettled feeling she'd experienced for the last forty-eight hours.

Time and anxiety suspended, and her thoughts floated away as she immersed herself in her one salvation—the joy of cooking.

She started on the caviar-topped bruschetta with ricotta and peppers while the parmigiana was in the last stages of cooking.

Setting it out on a sterling-silver tray, she headed upstairs to where the crew had set the table.

Her feet slowed when she saw the extra place setting, then she stopped completely at the intimacy created by the dim lighting and lit candles. Her stomach fluttered wildly as steel butterflies took flight inside her.

'Are you going to stand there all evening?' Narciso quipped from where he sat on a sofa that hugged the U-shape of the room.

'I...thought I was cooking for just you.'

'You thought wrong.' He stood, came over and pulled out her chair. 'Tonight we eat together.' His gaze took in her jeans. 'Right after you change.'

'I don't need to change.'

'One rule of business is to learn to let the little things slide. Standing on principle and antagonising your potential business partner doesn't make for a very good impression.'

'I really appreciate you helping me out but—'

'I would personally prefer not to eat with a dinner companion wearing clothes smeared with food.'

Ruby glanced down and, sure enough, a large oily streak had soiled her vest top.

He'd gone to the trouble of providing new clothes for her comfort. Would it hurt to show some appreciation? In a few days, she'd be back in New York, hopefully with a contract firmly in her pocket. He'd made it clear she was no longer attractive to him in the sexual sense, so she had nothing to fear there.

'I'll go and change,' she murmured around the disquiet spreading through her.

'*Grazie,*' he replied.

Returning to her suite, she quickly undressed and selected a soft peach, knee-length sundress with capped sleeves. Slipping her feet into three-inch wedged sandals, she tied her hair back and returned to the deck.

His gaze slid over her but his face remained neutral as he pulled out her chair.

'Sit, and tell me what you've made for us.'

The intimate *us* made her hand tremble. Taking a deep breath, she described the first course. He picked up a piece of bruschetta, slid it into his mouth and chewed.

The process of watching him eat something she'd made with her two hands was so strangely unsettling and erotic her fingers clenched on her napkin.

'Hmm, good enough.' He picked up another piece and popped it in his mouth.

When she found herself staring at his strong jaw and throat, she averted her gaze, picked up a piece and nibbled on the edge. 'Damned with faint praise.'

'The cracked pepper adds a zing. I like it.'

Heady pleasure flowed through her. 'Really?'

'I always mean what I say, Ruby.' His grave tone told her they weren't talking about just food.

'O...okay,' she answered. 'I have to check on the parmigiana in ten minutes.'

'That's more than enough time for a drink.'

Abandoning her half-eaten bruschetta, Ruby headed for the extensive bar, only to stop dead.

'We're no longer moored?' The bright lights of the marina had disappeared, leaving only the stunning dark orange of the setting sun as their backdrop.

'No, we're sailing along the coast. Tomorrow morning, I intend to dive the Blue Hole. Do you dive?' he asked.

She continued to the bar, her nerves jumpier than they had been a minute ago. 'I did, a long time ago.'

'Good. You'll join me.'

'Is that a request or a demand?'

He'd ignored her for the past two days. The idea that he now wanted to spend time with her jangled her fraying nerves. As she recalled what had happened on the plane heat and confusion spiked anew through her.

'It's a very civilised request.'

And yet...

Regardless of what Narciso was requesting, the last thing she needed to be doing was anticipating spending any time in his company. He made her lose control. She only had to look into his eyes to feel herself skating close to emotional meltdown.

The last thing she'd wanted when she met Narciso was to give in to the attraction she'd felt for him. But perversely, now he'd made it clear he intended to give her a wide berth, her mind kept conjuring up scenarios of how things could be between them.

She'd been wrong to compare Narciso to Simon, or even to her father. Despite the playboy exterior, she'd glimpsed a core of integrity in her potential new business partner that was markedly absent from the men she'd so far encountered.

Potential new business partner...

Therein lay her next problem. Whether active or passive, if she passed his test, Narciso would own a share in her business. They'd have a *business* relationship.

Which meant, nothing could be allowed to develop between them personally.

She worked almost absent-mindedly and only realised the drink she'd made after she opened the cocktail shaker. Aghast, she stared into the bold red drink.

'Are you going to serve...what is that anyway?'

Flames surged up her cheeks. 'Allow me to present the *Afrodisiaco.*'

One brow cocked; a touch of the irreverence she'd become used to darted over his features. 'Is there a message in there somewhere?'

That she'd produced one of the most suggestive cocktails on her list made her pulse jump as she poured it. 'It's just a name.'

He immediately shook his head. 'I've learned that nothing is ever what its face value suggests.' He sipped the cocktail, swirled it around in his mouth. 'Although now I've tasted this, I'm willing to alter that view.'

'Narciso…' The moment she uttered his name he froze. Another crack forked through the severely compromised foundation of her resistance as she watched his eyes darken.

'No, Ruby *mio,* you don't get to say my name for the first time like that.'

She paused. 'I'm sorry, but you need to explain to me what the last two days have been about.'

'*Basta…*' His voice held stark warning.

'*Non abbastanza!* I didn't ask you to seduce me on your plane. In fact, I made it very clear I wanted to be left alone because I knew   I wasn't… Look, whatever experiences you've had in the past are your own. But you told me you didn't like women who blew hot and cold. Well, guess what, that's exactly what you're doing!'

'Are you quite finished?' he grated out, his face a mask of taut control.

She gripped the counter until her knuckles whitened and she stared down at her dress. 'As a matter of fact, I'm not. Thank you for buying the clothes. If I appeared unappreciative before it was because I've learnt that nothing comes for free.'

'You're welcome,' he replied coolly. 'Now am I allowed to respond to that diatribe?'

'No. I have to check on the chicken parmagiana. The last thing I want to do is jeopardise my chances by serving you burnt food.' She rounded the bar and walked past him.

He grasped her wrist, easily imprisoning her.

Instantly, heat and electricity flooded through her. 'Let me go!'

'I haven't been blowing hot and cold.'

'You've certainly made avoiding me an art form.'

'I was trying to save us both from making a mistake, *tesoro.*'

The realisation that she didn't want that choice made for her sent a bolt of shock through her. Sheer self-preservation made her raise her chin. 'Well, you needn't have bothered. In fact you did me a favour back on your plane.'

His hand tightened. 'Really?'

'Yes. You reminded me that you're not my type.'

His nostrils flared. 'And how would you know what your type is considering your lack of experience?'

'I don't need experience to know playboys turn me off.'

His mouth flattened. 'You didn't seem turned off when you climaxed on top of me, then proceeded to writhe beneath me.'

The reminder made her pulse skitter. The hungry demand that hadn't abated since then made her pull harder. He set her free and she retreated fast. 'Maybe I wanted to see what the fuss was all about. Whatever. You helped me refocus on the reason I'm here on your boat. Now if you'll excuse me, I have to check on the main course.'

Narciso watched her go, furious that he'd allowed himself to be drawn into her orbit again.

The way he'd operated the last two days had been the best course.

So what if he'd climbed metaphoric walls while locked in his study? He'd sealed two deals and added to his billions, and he'd even managed to stop thinking about Ruby Trevelli for longer than five minutes.

But then his investigator had presented him with another opportunity to finish off Giacomo. And once again, Narciso had walked away, unable to halt the chain reaction inside that seemed to be scraping raw emotions he'd long ago suppressed; unable to stop his world hurtling towards a place he didn't recognise.

That his first thought had been to seek out Ruby and share his confusion had propelled him in the opposite direction.

His reaction to her continued to baffle him. In the last two days, he'd expended serious brainpower talking himself out of tracking down the woman who kissed like a seductress but whose innocence his conscience battled with him against tainting.

Dio, when the hell had he even *grown* a conscience?

With a growl, he grabbed the last of the canapés and munched on it. Delicate flavours exploded on his tongue.

The past two days had shown him how talented Ruby was in the kitchen and behind the bar. Her skill was faultless and she'd risen to his every challenge. In that time, while he'd locked himself in his study to resist temptation, he'd also reviewed the TV show footage and seen why she'd won the contest.

Her skittishness every time the camera had focused on her had also been made apparent.

She hated being under the spotlight. And yet she'd forced herself to do it, just so she could take control of her life.

His admiration for her had grown as he'd watched the footage even as he'd cursed at the knowledge that she was burrowing deeper under his skin.

He looked up as she entered, a silver-topped casserole dish in her hand. The flourish and expertise with which she set the dish down spoke of her pride in her work. He waited until she served them both before he took the first bite.

His hand tightened around his fork. 'Did you cook this for Simon?'

She visibly deflated. 'You don't like it.'

He didn't just like it. He loved it. So much so he was suddenly jealous of her sharing it with anyone else. 'I didn't say that. Did you cook it for him?'

Slowly, she shook her head.

Relief poured through him. 'Good.'

'So, you like it?' she asked again.

'*Sì,* very much,' he responded, his voice gruff.

The pleasure that lit up her face made his heart squeeze. He wanted to keep staring at her, bathe in her delight.

Dio, he was losing it.

He reached for the bottle to pour her a glass of chilled Chablis.

'No, thanks,' she said.

His hand tightened around the bottle. 'You have nothing to fear by drinking around me, Ruby.'

She raised her head and he saw a mixture of anguish and sadness displayed in her eyes. In that moment, Narciso wanted to hunt down the parents who'd done this to her and deliver unforgettable punishment.

'I know, but I'd like to keep a clear head, all the same.'

He set the wine aside and reached for the mineral water. 'Well, getting blind drunk on my own is no fun, so I guess we're teetotalling.'

She rolled her eyes and smiled, and his gut clenched hard.

'We haven't discussed wines yet. When we're done meet me at the upper deck. And wear a swimsuit. The sun may have gone down but you'll still boil out there in that dress.'

The tension in his body eased when she nodded.

After dinner, he made his way up to the deck. They could do this... They could have a conversation despite the spiked awareness of each other. Or the hunger that burned relentlessly through him—

Five minutes later, she mounted the stairs to the deck and his thoughts scattered.

Madre di Dio!

The body he could see beneath the sarong was spectacular. But he couldn't see enough of it. And he wanted to, despite the *off limits* signs he'd mentally slapped on her.

Seeing doesn't mean touching.

'Drop the sarong. You don't need it here.'

She fidgeted with the knot and his temperature rose higher. It loosened as she walked over to the lounger. She finally dropped it, sat down, and crossed her legs. Minutes ticked by. She re-crossed her legs.

'Stop fidgeting.'

She blew out a sigh. 'I can't stand the tension.'

'Well, running away won't make it go away.'

'I wasn't planning to run,' she replied. 'You wanted to talk about wines, remember?'

He nodded, although he'd lost interest in that subject. Forcing himself to look away from the temptation of the small waist that flared into very feminine hips and long, shapely legs, he stared at the moon rising over the water.

'Or I could easily return to my cabin and we can continue to treat each other like strangers.'

He considered the idea for exactly two seconds before he tossed it.

'What the hell, Ruby *mio*, let's give civility a try.'

She exhaled, sat up and poured a glass of mineral water from the jug nearby. 'Okay, first, I have to ask—what the heck is up with your name, anyway?'

He smiled despite the poker-sharp pain in his gut. 'You don't like it?'

'It's…different.'

'It was Giacomo's idea of a joke. But I've grown into it, don't you think?' Despite his joviality, the pain in his chest grew. Her eyes stayed on him and he saw when she noticed it. For some reason, revealing himself in that way didn't disturb him as much as he'd thought it would. In fact, talking to her soothed him.

'You've never wanted to change it?'

'It's just a name. I'm sure a few people will agree I can be narcissistic on occasion. I have no problems in pleasing number one.'

Her eyes gleamed with speculative interest. 'It really doesn't bother you, does it?'

'It may have, once upon a time,' he confessed. 'But not any more.'

Sympathy filled her eyes. 'I'm sorry.'

He tried to speak but words locked in his throat. Two simple words. Powerful words that calmed his roiling emotions. *'Grazie,'* he murmured.

His eyes caught and held hers. Something shifted, settled between them. An acknowledgement that neither of them were whole or without a history of buried hurt.

'The email on the plane. What was that about?' he asked abruptly.

She slowly inhaled. 'Before I tell you, promise me it won't

affect the outcome of this test run.' Her imploring look almost made him reply in the affirmative.

He hardened his resolve when he realised she was doing it again. Getting under his skin. Making a nonsense of his common sense.

'Sorry, *amante,* I don't make blind promises when it comes to business.'

Her lips firmed. 'Simon sold his share of the business to a guy who doesn't see eye to eye with my business plan.' In low tones, she elaborated.

He jerked upright. 'You're being threatened by a loan shark?'

'Yes.'

'And you didn't think to inform me?' he demanded.

'Would you have believed me? Especially in light of how I approached you?'

'Perhaps not right then, but…' The idea that he was prepared to give her the benefit of the doubt gave him a moment's pause. 'What's his name?'

'I don't know—he refused to tell me. All he wants is his money.'

'So I own twenty-five per cent of your business and a loan shark whose name you don't know another twenty-five per cent?'

'Yes.'

He slowly relaxed on his lounger and stared at her. 'You do realise that our agreement is transforming into substantially more than a talent-contest-prize delivery, don't you?'

A flush warmed her skin. 'I'm not sure I know what you mean.'

'What I mean, Ruby *mio,* is that in order to realise my twenty-five-per-cent investment, it seems I have to offer my business expertise. Writing you a cheque after next week and walking away is looking less and less likely.'

Why that thought pleased him so much, Narciso refused to examine.

CHAPTER EIGHT

'I DON'T REMEMBER the last time I sunbathed.'

'I can tell.'

Blue eyes glared at him and his pulse rocketed. Narciso tried to talk himself calmer. No one else was to blame since *he'd* invited her to go scuba-diving with him. *After* another sleepless night battling unrelenting sexual frustration.

'How can you tell? And don't tell me it's because you're a warlock.'

'I don't need otherworldly powers, *cara*. Your skin is so pale it's almost translucent and there are no visible tan lines.'

She glanced down at herself. 'Oh.'

'Here.' He grabbed the sun protection, started to move towards her, changed his mind at the last minute and tossed it to her.

'Thanks.' She sat on the same lounger as last night. But this time, the smell of her skin and the drying sea water made his blood heat.

'Where did you learn to dive?' he asked to distract himself from following the slim fingers that worked their way up her leg.

She smiled. 'I spent a few summers working at a hotel in Florida when I was in high school. I worked in the kitchens and got to dive in my spare time.'

'Have you always known you wanted to be a chef?'

Her smile immediately dimmed and he cursed himself for broaching a touchy subject.

'I knew I had my parents' talent but I resisted it for a long time.'

'I've seen the footage of the contest. You're not a natural in front of the camera.'

One brow rose. 'Gee, thanks.'

'What I mean is, you can easily prove to your parents that they're wasting their time trying to recruit you.'

'It won't stop them from trying.'

He shrugged. 'Then tell them you have a demanding new business partner.'

She shook her head. 'I'd rather not.'

'You want to keep me your dirty little secret, *tesoro?*'

She smiled but the light in her eyes remained dim. 'Something like that. What about you? Have you always known you wanted to be a warlock?'

He laughed, experiencing a new lightness inside. When her lips curved in response, he forcibly clenched his hands to stop from reaching for her. 'Ever since I made my first million at eighteen.'

'Wow, that must have brought the girls running.'

He shrugged, suddenly reluctant to dwell on past conquests. 'It gave me the ammunition I needed...'

She frowned slightly. 'Ammunition. To fight your father?'

'To fight Giacomo, yes.'

'Why do you call him Giacomo?'

He exhaled. 'Because he was never a *father* to me.'

She paused and that soft look entered her eyes. The realisation that he didn't mind talking to her about his past shocked him. He tried to tell himself it meant nothing, but he knew he was deluding himself.

'What about your mother? Is she alive?'

Sharp pain pierced his chest. 'My poor mama is what started this whole nasty business.'

'What do you mean?'

'She died giving birth to me. I was so determined to make

a quick entrance into the world, I caused her to bleed almost to death by the roadside before an ambulance could arrive.'

Her gasp echoed around the sun-dappled deck. 'Surely, you don't think that's your fault?'

'Giacomo certainly seems to think so.'

It occurred to him that Ruby was the first woman he'd actively conversed with. Normally, any conversation was limited to the bedroom. But with sex off the table it seemed *talking* was the next best thing.

'That's why there's so much animosity between you two. He blames you for your mother's death?'

'It may have started out that way, but our *relationship* has evolved…mutated.'

'Into what?'

He started to answer then stopped. 'Into something that's no longer clear-cut.' Shock rolled through him as he accepted the truth. He'd started out wanting to destroy his father. Along the way, and especially lately, the urge to deliver the kill blow had waned. Even toying with his father now no longer held any interest for him.

'So what are you going to do about it?'

Sì, what was he going to do?

Call it a day and cut off all ties with Giacomo? The sudden ache in his gut made him stiffen and jerk upright.

'Enough about me. You have an exceptional talent. I'm officially hiring you to cater my dinner party.'

The compliment brought a smile to her lips. Again, he forced himself not to reach out and caress the satin smoothness of her determined jaw. The urge was stronger because he needed something to blot out his confused thoughts of his father.

'Thank you.' She put the sun protection down and glanced at him. 'Can I get you anything?'

He shook his head. 'No more cocktails.'

Her smile widened. 'Then I have the perfect thing.'

She stood and walked to the chiller behind the bar. To his

surprise she returned with an ice-cold beer. 'Sometimes a beer is the perfect solution to thirst.'

Narciso twisted off the cap with relish and took a long swig, and looked over to find her eyes on his throat. The feel of her eyes on him made his temperature shoot sky-high.

'Aren't you having a drink?'

She indicated the glass of water on the table next to her lounger.

'That must be warm by now.'

Wordlessly, he held out the bottle to her. Her eyes met his and sensation skated over him. Their attraction was skittering out of control but he couldn't seem to apply the brakes.

'You're thirsty. Take it.'

Slowly, she took the bottle from him. Her pink tongue darted out to caress the lip of the bottle before she took a small swig.

She held it back out to him. 'Thanks.'

'So beers are an exception to your don't-drink-much rules?'

'A small drink doesn't hurt.'

'Aren't you afraid you'll lose control with me?' he asked roughly.

'We established that anything between us would be a mistake, remember?'

He stepped deeper into quicksand, felt it close dangerously over him but still he didn't retreat.

Eyes on her, he took another swig of beer. 'Perhaps that no longer holds true.'

Her breath audibly hitched. 'Why? Tell me and I'll remind you when things threaten to get out of hand.'

He couldn't stop the laughter that rumbled from his chest. 'You mean as some form of shock therapy?'

'If it's what works for you.'

His gaze slid down her body. Skin made vibrant by the sun and the exertions of their dive this morning offered temptation so strong it was no wonder he could think straight.

'Don't worry, *tesoro,* I'll try and curb my uncontrollable urges.'

'I'm glad you can. I'm not so sure about myself,' she blurted.

For a moment, he thought his hearing was impaired. 'What did you just say?'

She shut her eyes and cursed as he'd only heard a true New Yorker curse. 'I feel as if I'm skidding close to the edge of my control where you're concerned. After Simon—'

'I am *not* Simon,' he grated out.

She trembled. 'Believe me, I know. But even though I keep telling myself what a bad idea this is, I can't stop myself from… wanting you.'

The blunt delivery made his eyes widen. 'You realise how much power you're giving me by telling me?'

'Yes. But I'm hoping you won't take undue advantage of it.'

Slowly, he set the bottle down. 'Come here.'

'Did I not just mention undue advantage?'

'Come here and we'll see if the advantage is undue or not.'

Ruby stood slowly and stepped towards him, fighting for a clear breath as he loomed large, powerful and excruciatingly addictive before her. Her skin burned where he cradled her hips in his palms.

'What do you want, Ruby?' he rasped.

She looked into his face and every self-preservation instinct fled.

She'd never met a man like Narciso Valentino before. Everything she'd found out about him in the last few days had blown her expectations of him sky-high.

His name might indicate self-absorption but she was learning he was anything but. He could've reported her to Zeus when he'd found out she'd applied to be a *Petit Q* under false pretences. He could've sent her packing after she told him about his company owing her. Stopping himself from seducing her and his generosity with the clothes coupled with his easy companionship this morning as they'd scuba-dived at one of the most beautiful places in the world had shown her that Narciso could be nothing like his name.

Little by little, the traits she'd discovered had whittled at her defences.

And now…

'As crazy and stupid as it is, I want to kiss you more than I want to breathe.'

Dear God, what was wrong with her?

'*Dio mio.*' He sounded strained…disarmed, as if she'd knocked his feet from under him.

She ought to pull back, retreat to the safety of her cabin. Instead, she took his face in her hands, leaned forward and kissed him.

His grunt of desire slammed into her before he seized her arms. Leaning back against the lounger, he tugged her on top of him. Strong arms imprisoned her as he moulded her body to his.

The evidence of arousal against her belly was unmistakable, gave her strength she hadn't known existed. She plunged her tongue into his mouth, felt the stab of pleasure when he jerked beneath her and groaned long and deep.

Firm hands angled her head for a deeper penetration that made her pulse thud a hundred times faster.

He made love to her with his mouth, lapping at her lips with long strokes that pulled at the hot, demanding place between her legs.

Her hands hungrily explored his warm, firm muscle and hair-roughened chest. When her fingers encountered his nipple, she grazed her nail against it, the way she knew drove him mad.

He tore his mouth from hers, his eyes molten grey as he gazed up at her.

'*Cara mia*, this will not end well for either of us if you don't stop that.'

Brazenly, she repeated the action. And watched in fascination as it puckered and goose bumps rose around the hard disc. Before she could give in to the urge to taste it, Narciso was moving her higher, stark purpose on his face.

'One bad turn deserves another.' Roughly, he tugged at her

bikini string and caught one plump breast in his mouth as they were freed from the garment.

The sight of him feasting on her in the dimming light was so erotic, Ruby's nails dug into his chest.

Her hips bucked against his hardness, that hunger climbing even higher as she rubbed against his full, heavy thickness. The thought of having that power inside her made her whimper. When his teeth tugged at her in response, her moan turned into a cry.

Foolish or not, dangerous or not, she wanted him. More than she'd ever wanted anything in her life. For the first time, Ruby understood a little bit of the passion that drove her parents. Of the need that forced two people wholly unsuited to stay together. If it was anywhere near this addictive, this mad, she could almost sympathise…

'Narciso…please…'

One hand splayed over her bottom, squeezed before grabbing the stretchy material of her bikini. He pulled, sending a million stars bursting behind her closed eyelids as the pressure on her heated clitoris intensified her pleasure. At her shocked gasp, he pulled tighter. Liquid heat rushed to fill her sensitive flesh. Almost immediately, she needed more, so much more that her body was threatening to burst out of her skin. She sank her hands into his hair and bit down on the rough skin of his jaw.

He cursed and froze, hard fingers gripping her hips. When the sensation slid from pleasure to a hint of pain, she lifted her head to gaze drowsily at him.

'What…?'

'Before this goes any further I need to be sure you want this,' he rasped.

She looked down, saw her state of undress, saw his hard, ready body.

Instinctively she went to adjust her clothes, her face flushing with heat. 'God, what's wrong with me?'

He stopped her agitated movements with steady hands. 'Hey,

there's *nothing* wrong with you. You're a sensual creature, with natural needs just like—'

'My father?' she inserted bleakly.

Surprisingly gentle hands framed her face. 'If you were like him you wouldn't still be a virgin. Do you get that?'

Tears prickled her eyes. 'But...I...'

'No, no more excuses. You stopped being their puppet a long time ago—you just forgot to cut the strings.'

Her breath stalled and her vision blurred. He brushed away her tears and she fought to speak. 'What does that say about me?'

His jaw clenched. 'That we sometimes spend too much time looking in the rear-view mirror to see what's ahead.'

She moved on top of him because, despite everything going south, her hunger hadn't abated one iota. His hands clamped down harder on her hips.

'What's in your rear-view mirror?' she asked him softly.

'Too much. Much too much.'

His answer held a depth of anguish that cut to her soul. Heart aching for him, she started to lean down but he caught and held her still.

'No.'

She looked into his face and saw his slightly ashen pallor. 'You don't want me to kiss you?'

His chest heaved and he glanced away.

The realisation hit her like a bolt of lightning. 'You stopped us making love on the plane and just now because you don't think you're worth it, do you? Why not? Because your father told you you weren't?'

'Ruby, stop,' he warned.

She ignored him, the need to offer comfort bleeding through her. She caressed his taut cheek. A pulse beat so hard in his jaw, her fingers tingled from the contact.

'*Cara,* I'm a man on the edge. A man who wants what he shouldn't have. Get off me before I do something we'll both regret, *per favore.*'

Fresh tears prickled her eyes, stung the back of her throat.

If anyone had told her a week ago she'd be lying on top of the world's most notorious playboy, baring her soul to him and catching a glimpse of his ragged soul in return, she'd have called them insane.

Her hands shook as she slowly removed them from his face. Levering herself away from him was equally hard because her knees rebelled at supporting her in her weakened state.

Snatching at her bikini top, desperately trying to ignore his silent scrutiny, she tied the strings as best she could and secured the sarong over her chest.

Her hair was an unruly mess she didn't bother to tackle. What had just happened had gone beyond outer appearances.

She looked down at him and he returned her look, the torture unveiled now. She floundered, torn between helping him and fleeing to examine her own confused emotions. Eventually, she chose the latter. 'I have a few things to take care of in the kitchen before I go to bed. *Bona notti.*'

Slowly, he rose to tower over her, and in the fading daylight she saw his bunched fists at his sides.

His smile was cut from rough stone. 'I've awakened too many demons for me to have a restful night, *tesoro*. But I wish you a good night all the same.'

I've awakened too many demons...

Ruby lay in bed a few hours later, wracked with guilt.

She'd pushed him to relive his past, to rake over old wounds because she'd wanted to know the real man underneath the gloss.

To reassure herself he wouldn't hurt or betray her?

Shame coiled through her as she acknowledged that she'd been testing him. But then deep down, ever since he'd turned away from her on the plane, she'd known Narciso was nothing like her father. Or Simon.

And still she'd pushed...

She reared up and gripped the side of her bed. Her head

cautioned her against the need to find out if she'd pushed him too far, if the demons were indeed keeping him awake. But her heart propelled her to her feet.

She went down the hallway and knocked on his door before her courage deserted her.

The evidence that he was indeed up came a second later when the door was wrenched open. He was dressed in his silk pajama bottoms and nothing else.

'What the hell are you doing here, Ruby?' he flung at her.

She struggled to look up from his chest. 'I…wanted to make sure you were okay. And to apologise for what happened earlier. I had no right to push you like that.'

His eyes narrowed for several seconds before he turned and strode back into the bedroom. 'I'm learning that warlocks and demons keep good company.' He picked up a crystal tumbler of Scotch, raised it to her and took a sip.

Ruby found herself moving forward before she'd consciously made the decision to.

Her hand closed over the glass and stopped his second sip.

He stepped back away from her but, hampered by the bed, he abruptly sank down. She took the glass from him and set it on the side table.

'Drinking is not the answer. Trust me, I know.'

Strong hands gripped the sheets as if physically stopping himself from reaching for her and he exhaled harshly.

This close, the beauty of him took her breath away. His chest heaved again, the movement emphasising his stunning physique and golden skin.

Fiery desire slammed into her so hard she reeled under the onslaught.

Before she could stop to question herself, she slid her hands over his biceps. Warm muscles rippled under her touch.

'What the hell are you doing?' His voice was rough and gritty with need.

Her face flamed but a deeper fire of determination burned

within her. 'I have a feeling it's called seduction. I don't know because I've never done this before.'

She leaned in closer. He groaned as her hardened T-shirt-covered nipples grazed his chest. '*Per amore di Dio,* why are you doing it now?'

She placed a finger over his lip and felt a tiny jolt of triumph when it puckered slightly against her touch. 'Because it's driving me as insane. And because I don't want to live in fear of what I might become if I let go. So this is me owning my fear.'

He cursed again and he shook his head. Knowing he was about to deny her, she pushed him onto the bed and sealed her mouth over his.

He groaned and accepted her kiss with a demanding roughness that threatened to blow her away. Encouraged by that almost helpless response, she threw one leg over him and straddled his big body.

Immediately, his already potent arousal thickened, lengthened, found the cradle between her legs. Before she lost her mind completely, Ruby reached out to both sides of the bed and loosened the ties she needed, then she worked quickly before he could stop her.

He wrenched his mouth from hers, and glanced up. Silver eyes darkening in shock, then disbelief. '*Hai perso la tua mente?*'

'No, I haven't lost my mind.'

'Clearly, you have.' He yanked on the binds but they only tightened further. 'Release me, Ruby.'

'Nope. What goes around comes around, *tesoro.*'

Feeling a little bit bolder now she knew he wouldn't easily overpower her or dismiss her, she took a deep breath, drew her T-shirt over her head and flung it away.

'Ruby...' Warning tinged his low growl.

She wavered but the look in his eyes stalled her breath— hunger, anger, a touch of admiration, that little bit of wonder and vulnerability she'd seen earlier on the deck all mingled in his hypnotic eyes.

'I would, but the look in your eyes is scaring me right now. What's to say you won't devour me the minute I set you free?' She trailed a finger down his chest and revelled in his hitched breathing.

'I won't,' he bit out.

She shivered again at the menace in his voice. 'Liar, liar.'

'*Madre di Dio,* do you really want to lose your virginity so badly?'

She shook her head and her hair came free from the loose knot she'd put it into. 'No, it isn't actually that important to me. What I want, what I crave, is to make love with you.'

His eyes darkened. 'Why?'

She tamped down on what she really wanted to say. That he'd shown her another way to view herself. Another way that didn't make her skin crawl for feeling sensual pleasure.

'Do I have to have some noble reason? Isn't crazy chemistry enough? I was absolutely fine before you touched me. You woke this hunger inside me. Now because of some stupid principle, you're trying to deny me what I want. What we both want. I won't let you.'

His chest heaved. 'I won't let you either. Not like this.' The roughness in his tone gave her pause. When she looked into his eyes, that bleakness she'd spotted in the kitchen on their first morning in Macau was back. 'If you want me, release me.'

She wanted to kiss that look away, to utterly and totally eradicate it so it never returned. Leaning down, she did exactly that, luxuriating in the velvety feel of his warm lips. He kissed her back but she could sense the agitation clawing under his skin and she drew back a little. Caressing his chest and shoulders, she touched her lips to his again in a gentle offer of solace from whatever demons were eating him alive.

A rough sigh rumbled from his chest.

'Narciso…'

His lips trembled against hers. 'Release me, Ruby.'

Heart in her throat, she repeated the words he'd said to her in Macau. 'I already have.'

Shocked eyes darted upward. A split second later he was flipping her beneath him, ripping away her panties and flinging them over his shoulder.

Molten eyes speared her as he tugged off his pyjamas, his gaze settling possessively on her damp, exposed sex. 'Sorry, Ruby *mio,* I lied.'

'About what?' Her voice trembled.

'About not devouring you.'

Hot, sensual lips grazed down her cleavage to her navel, the rasp of his growing stubble sending electrifying tingles racing through her body. His tongue circled her navel, then strong teeth bit the skin just below.

Her shudder threatened to lift her off the bed.

One large hand splayed on her stomach and the other parted her legs wider. Watching him watch her was the most erotic experience of her life so far.

She didn't need a crystal ball to know there was more, so much more in store for her.

He bypassed her most sensitive place, lifted one leg to bend it at the knee. Hot kisses trailed down her inside thigh. Again the graze of his stubble added a rough, pleasurable edge that made her breath come out in agitated gasps.

Nibbling his way down, he soothed his bites with open-mouthed kisses that sparked a yearning for that mouth at her core.

But he took his time. Leisurely, he kissed his way down her other thigh, all the while widening her thighs, those molten eyes not leaving her heated sex.

Ruby wondered why she wasn't dying with embarrassment. But seeing the effect the sight of her had on him—nostrils flared as he breathed her in, his fingers trembling slightly as he gripped her knee—she had little room for anything but desire.

'Lei è sfarzoso,' he muttered thickly.

She *felt* gorgeous, a million miles from what she'd always feared she would feel when it came to sex. She blinked back tears and cried out as sublime pleasure roared through her.

Lips, tongue, teeth. True to his words Narciso devoured her with a singular, greedy purpose.

From far away, she heard her cries of ecstasy, smelled the heat of his skin coupled with the scent of her arousal as she writhed with bliss beneath him.

Just when she thought she would burst out of her skin, he raised his head.

'I'd had this thought in my head that the first time I took you I'd torture you for hours with pleasure.' Still holding her down, he pulled open the beside drawer and grabbed a condom. Impatiently, he ripped it open with his teeth. 'But I can't wait one more second, *amante*.'

'I don't want you to.'

Hooded eyes regarded her. 'I can't promise it will be gentle. I could hurt you.'

The slight note of apprehension washed away when she recalled what had happened on the deck earlier this evening. Despite the volatile emotions that had raged between them, he'd never hurt her.

She laid her hand over the one he'd flattened on her belly. 'I'm ready.'

He leaned back and she saw him, really saw him for the first time. The erection that sprang from his groin was powerful and proud. Another testament to how well his name suited him. Judging from the size of him, he had a lot to crow about in that department, too.

Holding himself in one fist, he rolled on the condom and settled stormy eyes on her. 'Are you sure about this?' he rasped.

'Right this moment, my confidence is wavering a little,' she confessed, her voice shaky with the knowledge that he would soon be inside her.

He inhaled deeply. 'I promise to go as fast or as slow as you desire,' he said in a deep solemn voice.

Unable to speak, Ruby nodded. In a slow, predatory crawl he surged over her. Dark hair fell over his forehead in that careless way she found irresistible. She had a second to weave her fingers through it before he was kissing her again.

By the time he lifted his head hers was swimming. The flush that scoured his cheekbones signalled his fast-slipping control. His erection pulsed against her thigh and the very air crackled with sensual expectation so thick, all her confidence from minutes ago oozed out of her like air from a balloon.

'What do I do now?'

He glanced down to where her hunger raged, to the glistening entrance to her body. 'Open wider for me,' he breathed.

Every single atom in her body poised with tingling expectation as she complied with his command and spread her thighs wider. 'Now what?'

Silver eyes returned to hers. 'Now...you breathe, Ruby *mio*.' He took her lips in a quick, hard kiss. 'This will be no fun at all if you pass out.'

Reeling from the sensation coursing through her, she sucked air through her mouth.

'That's it. Eyes on me and don't move,' he instructed.

The first push inside her threatened to expel the air she'd fed her starving lungs. From head to toe, Ruby was soaked in indescribable sensation.

'Oh!' She breathed out again, her hands tightening on his shoulders as her craving escalated. 'More.'

He shut his eyes for a split second, then he pushed in further, carefully gauging her reaction as he deepened the penetration.

The need clawing through her sharpened, deepened. Unable to lie still, she twisted upward to meet him.

'*Dio!* Don't do that.'

'But I like it.' She twisted higher, then gave a cry as pain ripped through her pelvis.

'*Per amore di...* I told you not to move.' His lips were tension-white and sweat beaded his forehead.

He started to withdraw but the pain was already fading. Quickly she clamped her legs around his waist.

'No.' He levered his arms on either side of her in preparation to remove himself from her body. The knowledge that he was holding himself back so forcefully sent a different sensation through her.

Her hand trailed up his throat to clutch his nape, holding him prisoner. 'Yes.'

Tightening her grip, she forced her hips up. He slid deeper to fully embed himself within her and she cried out in pleasure. 'Ruby…'

'Make love to me, Narciso,' she pleaded, because she knew that whatever she was feeling right now, there was so much more to come. 'Please.'

With a groan, he sealed his body fully with hers.

Sizzling pleasure raced up her spine as he set a thrusting rhythm designed to drive her out of her mind. Considering she was already halfway there, it didn't take long before Ruby stopped breathing again, poised on the edge of some unknown precipice that beckoned with seductive sorcery.

Against her lips, Narciso murmured thick, hot words in native Sicilian. Those that she understood would've made her blush if her whole body wasn't already burning from the fierce power of his possession.

His lips grazed along her jaw, down her throat to enslave one nipple in his mouth. His tongue lapped her in rhythm with his thrusts, adding another dimension to the sensations flowing through her.

One hand hooked under her thigh, spreading her even wider. He groaned at the altered angle just as she began to fracture.

He raised his head from her breast and locked his gaze on hers. The connection, deep, hot and direct, was the final straw.

Convulsions tore through her, rocking her from head to toe with indescribable bliss that wrenched a scream from the depths of her soul.

Lost in the maelstrom of ecstasy, she heard him groan deeply before long shudders seized his frame.

His damp forehead touched hers, then his head found the

curve of her shoulder. Hot, agitated breaths bathed her neck as his heartbeat thundered in tandem with hers.

In that moment, she experienced a closeness she'd never experienced with another human being. She told herself it was a false sensation but still she basked in it, unable to stop the giddy, happy feeling washing over her. Her arms tightened around him and she would gladly have stayed there for ever but he moved, turning sideways to lie on the bed.

'I don't want to crush you.' His voice was thick, almost gruff.

'Don't worry, I'm stronger than I look.'

He half growled. 'I guessed as much earlier. Where did you learn to make ties like that?'

'Tying up chickens and turkeys for roasting.'

He grimaced. 'I'm flattered.'

'Don't worry, Narciso. I'll never mistake you for a chicken.'

His laughter caused her heart to soar, the simple pleasure of making him laugh lifting her spirits.

Resting her chin on his chest, she looked into his eyes. *'Grazie.'*

He caught a curl and twisted it around his finger. *'Per quello che?'*

'For making my first so memorable.'

'It was a first for me, too, after a fashion.'

A thousand questions smashed through her brain but she forced herself to push them away. 'Hmm, I guess it was.'

They lay in replete silence for several more minutes. And then the atmosphere began to change.

She started to move but his arm tightened around her. A deep swallow moved his Adam's apple.

'Tomorrow, we'll talk properly, *sì?'*

Heart in her throat, she nodded. *'Sì.'*

'Good. Now I get to show you my favourite knot.'

CHAPTER NINE

'*Ciao.*'

The deep voice roused her from languor and she opened her eyes to find Narciso standing over her lounger, cell phone in one hand.

The midmorning sun blazed on the private deck outside his bedroom suite and Ruby squirmed under his gaze as it raked her.

'*Ciao.* I can't believe I let you convince me to sunbathe nude.'

'Not completely nude.' He eyed her bikini bottoms.

Heat crawled up her neck and she hurriedly changed the subject. 'Was your call successful?'

'*Sì,* but then all my negotiations are,' he said with a smug smile.

'Your modesty is so refreshing. I guess making a million dollars by age eighteen tends to go to one's head.'

'On the contrary, my head was very clear. I had only one goal in mind.'

Despite the sun's blaze, she shivered. 'So it started that long ago, this feud between you two?'

He tossed his phone onto the table and stretched out on the lounger next to hers. Ruby fought not to ogle the broad, firm expanse of skin she'd taken delight in exploring last night. The grim look on his face helped her resist the temptation.

'Believe it or not, there was a time when I toyed with the idea of abandoning it.'

Surprise scythed through her. 'Really?'

'*Sì,*' he replied, almost inaudibly.

'What happened?'

'I graduated from Harvard a year early and decided to spend my gap year in Sicily. I knew Giacomo would be there. And I knew he couldn't throw me out because the house he lived in belonged to my mother and she'd willed it to me when I turned eighteen. I...hoped that being under the same roof again for the first time in five years would give us a different perspective.'

'It didn't?'

The hand on his thigh slowly curled into a fist. 'No. We clashed harder than ever.'

She couldn't mistake the ragged edge in his voice. 'If he hated you being there so much, why didn't he leave?'

'That would've meant I'd won. Besides, he took pleasure in reminding me I'd killed my mother on the street right outside her home.'

Ice drenched her veins. 'What happened to her?'

'She suffered a placental abruption three weeks before I was due. She'd gone for a walk and was returning home. By the time she dragged herself up the road to the house to alert anyone, she'd lost too much blood. Apparently, the doctor said he could only save one of us. Giacomo asked him to save my mother. She died anyway. I survived.'

Ruby reached out and covered his fist with her hand. He tensed for a second, then his hand wrapped around hers.

'How can anyone in their right mind believe that something so tragic was your fault?'

'Giacomo believed it. That was enough. And he was right to demand that the doctor save my mother.'

She flinched. 'How can you say that?'

'Because he knew what I would become.'

'A wildly successful businessman who donates millions of dollars each year to fund neo-natal research among other charitable organisations?'

He jerked in surprise. 'How do you know that?'

A blush crept up her cheeks. 'When I did a web search on you a few things popped up.'

He shrugged. 'My accountants tell me funding charities is a good way to get tax breaks. Don't read more into the situation than there is, *amante*.'

Lowering her gaze, she watched their meshed fingers. The feel of his skin against hers made her heart skip several beats. 'I think we're past the point where you can convince me you're all bad, Narciso,' she dared.

He remained silent for so long she thought he'd refused to pick up the thread of their conversation. Then his breath shuddered out. 'Giacomo believes that.'

'Because you perpetuate that image?'

His smile was grim but it held speculation. 'Perhaps, but it's an image I'm growing tired of.'

Her breath caught.

His eyes met hers and he reached across and took her hand. 'Does that surprise you? That I'm thinking it's time to end this vendetta?'

'Why the change of heart?' she asked.

His casual shrug looked a little stiff. 'Perhaps it's time to force another mutation of our relationship,' he said obliquely.

'And if it fails?'

His eyes darkened before his lashes swept down to veil his expression. 'I'm very good at adapting, *amante*.' He stood up abruptly and pulled her up. 'Time for a shower.'

She waited until they were both naked in the bedroom before she spoke.

'All that with Giacomo. I'm sorry it happened to you.'

His nostrils flared as bleakness washed over his face. Then slowly, he reasserted control.

Intense silver eyes travelled over her, lingering on her bare breasts with fierce hunger that made her nipples pucker. 'Don't be. Our feud brought me to Macau. Macau brought you to me. I call that a win-win situation, *amante*.'

He lunged up and grabbed her. Swinging her up in his arms, he crossed the suite and entered the adjoining bathroom.

'Wait, we haven't finished talking.'

'*Sì,* we have. I've revealed more of my past to you than to any other living soul. If I'm The Warlock you should be re-named The Sorceress.'

Demanding hands reached for her, propelled her backwards into the warm shower he'd turned on.

'But I don't know you nearly enough.'

He yanked the shower head from its cradle and aimed the nozzle in the curve of her neck. Water set to the perfect tem-perature soothed her and she allowed her mind to slide free of the questions that raced through her thoughts.

Understanding the boy he'd been, caught in the hell of a fa-ther who hated the very sight of him, Ruby found it wasn't a stretch to understand why he'd closed himself off.

But she'd seen beneath the façade, knew the playboy persona was just a defence mechanism. His relationship with Giacomo meant more to him than he was willing to admit.

As if reading her thoughts, he sent her a narrow-eyed glare. 'Don't try and *understand* me, Ruby. You may not like what you discover.'

'What's that supposed to mean?'

His eyes met hers and she glimpsed the dark river of anguish. 'It means there may never be enough underneath the surface to be worth your time.'

'Shouldn't I be the judge of that?'

He stepped forward and aimed the shower right between her thighs. Ruby gasped as sensation weakened her knees. She reached out for something to steady her and got a handful of warm, vibrant flesh. He angled the showerhead and she let out a strangled moan.

'No. This conversation is over, *amante,*' he growled. 'Now, open wider for me.'

Despite his clipped words of warning and the blatantly sex-ual way he chose to end their conversation, Narciso proceeded to wash her with an almost worshipful gentleness that undid her. When he sank down in front of her and washed between her legs, tears prickled her eyes.

Hell, she was losing her mind. Right from the beginning, she'd primed herself to hate this skilled playboy for his shallow feelings and careless attitude towards women and sex.

Instead she'd discovered that beneath the glossy veneer lurked a wounded soul, hurting from a tortured past.

She wanted to touch him the way he'd touched her. She reached out, but he grasped her hand in his, surged upright and set the showerhead back in its cradle. Beside the expensive gels and lotions a stack of condoms rested. Her heart lurched as she saw him reach for one and tear it open.

Grasping her waist, he whirled her around, then meshed his fingers through hers before raising them to rest above her head.

'*This* is the only conversation I want to continue. Are you ready?' he rasped low in her ear.

His thickness pressed against her bottom. Recalling the pleasure she'd experienced before, she could no more stop herself from answering in the affirmative than she could stop herself from breathing.

He slid slowly into her, leaving her ample time to adjust to his size. Pleasure shot through her, imprisoning her in its merciless talons.

Her groan mingled with his as steam rose around and engulfed them in a cocoon of rough kisses and wet bodies.

Narciso let pleasure wash over him, erasing, if only temporarily, the cutting pain of the past rehashed. The raw agony of recollection eased as he surged deeper into her and, even though he refused to acknowledge that her touch, her warmth and soft words eased his pain, he hung on to the feel of being in her arms.

She rewarded him by crying out as her muscles tightened around him.

Dio mio, she was unbelievable! And she'd got under his skin with minimum effort. But he'd get his control back.

He had to.

Because this unravelling, as much as it soothed the deep wound in his heart, couldn't continue. For now, though, he intended to lose his mind in the most spectacular way. He slid his hands down her sides, glorying in her supple wet skin. Encircling her tiny waist, he threw his head back and let desire roar through his body.

She woke to a silent room and a half-cold bed.

Ruby didn't need a crystal ball to know regret played a part in Narciso's absence. She felt equally exposed and vulnerable in the light of day at how they'd bared their pasts to each other.

But as much as she wanted to stay hidden beneath the covers, she forced herself to leave Narciso's bed. Shoving her hand through her hair, she picked up the T-shirt she'd brazenly discarded during her seduction routine. Her ripped-beyond-redemption panties she quickly balled up in her fist.

Luckily, she met no one on the way to her own cabin.

Ten minutes later, and freshly showered, she dressed in white shorts and a sea-green sleeveless top, and opened her door to find a steward waiting outside.

'Mr Valentino would like you to join him for breakfast on the first deck.'

Her pulse raced as trepidation filled her.

Yesterday morning hadn't really counted as *the morning after* because after their shower they'd returned to bed and spent the rest of the day making love.

She entered the salon that led to the sun-dappled dining space on the deck.

Fresh croissants, coffee, juices and two domed dishes had been neatly laid out. But her attention riveted on the man flicking his finger across his electronic tablet.

'Morning,' she said, her voice husky.

His gaze rose and caught hers. 'Feeling rested?'

She managed a nod and glanced around. 'Where are we?' The day before they'd moored at the Bay of Placencia after leaving the spectacular Blue Hole.

'We're just coming into Nicholas Caye. Mexico is just north of us.'

'It's beautiful here,' she said, nerves eating her alive at the intense look in his eyes.

'Sit down and relax, Ruby. It will be hard but I can just about stop myself from jumping on you and devouring you for breakfast.'

Heat shot into her cheeks. 'That wasn't what I was thinking,' she blurted, then pursed her lips and pulled out a chair.

Lifting the dome, she found her favourite breakfast laid out in exquisite presentation. Along with her preferred spear of asparagus. 'You made me Eggs Benedict?' Why the hell was her throat clogged by that revelation?

'I didn't make it myself, *tesoro*. I'm quite useless in the kitchen.'

But he'd taken note somewhere along the way that this was her favourite breakfast meal. 'I... Thank you.'

He snapped shut his tablet, shook out his napkin and laid it over his lap. 'Don't read anything into it, Ruby.'

'You keep saying that. And yet you can't seem to help yourself with your actions.'

He picked up his cutlery. 'I must be losing my edge,' he muttered.

'Or maybe you're rediscovering your human side?'

He smiled mockingly. 'Now I sound like a reformed comic villain.'

'No, that would require a lot of spandex,' she quipped before taking a bite of the perfectly cooked eggs.

He laughed, the sound rich and deep. Ruby barely stopped the food from going down the wrong way when she glimpsed the gorgeously carefree transformation of his face. 'You don't think I'd look good in spandex?' he asked drily.

'I think you'd look good in anything. And I also believe you can do anything you put your mind to.'

He tensed and slowly lowered his knife. 'Is there a hidden message in that statement?'

'No…maybe. This is my first morning-after conversation. I may say things that aren't thought through properly.'

Her gaze connected with his. An untold wealth of emotions swirled through his eyes and her stomach flipped her heart into her throat. 'Now you're selling yourself short. You're one of the most talented, intelligent people I know,' he delivered. 'And the waters are treacherous for me, too.'

'Really?' she whispered.

His lids lowered, breaking the connection. '*Sì*. I think we both know we're under each other's skin. It's up to us to decide what we do with that knowledge. What's your most prized ingredient?'

'The white Alba truffle, hands down,' she blurted, reeling at the abrupt question. 'Truffles make everything taste better.'

He slowly nodded. '*Bene.*' He said nothing else and resumed eating.

Ruby felt as if she'd fallen down the rabbit hole again. The conversation felt surreal. 'Why is that important?'

His jaw clenched slightly. 'I need a truffles day to make me feel better.'

'Why?'

'Because I can't wrap my mind around the things I spilled to you yesterday.'

'I didn't force anything out of you, Narciso.'

'Which makes it even more puzzling. So I need a minute and you're going to give it to me,' he stated blatantly.

'How?'

'We're going to spend the day together. And you're going to tell me every single thought that jumps into your head.'

Her brows rose. 'You want to use me to drown out your thoughts? You realise how unhealthy that sounds, right?'

His grimace was pained. 'Yes, I do, but I'll suffer through it this once in the hope I emerge unscathed.'

'And if you don't?'

Silver eyes darkened as they swept over her. The message in

them when they locked on her lips punched heat into her belly. 'Then I'll have to find a different solution.'

Six hours later, Narciso was wondering if he'd truly lost his mind. Although he'd learned everything about Ruby from the moment she'd learned to speak to the present she'd received from her roommate, Annie, on her last birthday, he yearned to know more.

Never had he taken even the remotest interest in a woman besides her favourite restaurant and what pleased her in bed. The fact that he wanted to know Ruby Trevelli's every thought sent a shiver of apprehension down his spine.

He was unravelling faster than he could keep things under control.

Every emotion he'd tried to lock down since that summer in Sicily threatened to swamp him. He gritted his teeth and watched Ruby surge out of the turquoise sea. She walked towards him, clad in the minuscule bikini he'd supplied her with. Her body—supple, curvy and dripping with water—made his mouth dry. When she dropped down next to him on the deserted beach they'd swum to, he burned with the need to reach for her. *Dio,* with the amount of sex they'd had how could he still be this hungry for her?

'So, is the inquisition over?' she asked playfully.

'*Sì,*' he growled. 'It's over.'

Her gaze darted to his and he saw her tense at the coolness in his voice.

'Something wrong?'

'Why would anything be wrong?'

'Because you won the swim race from the yacht and you're not crowing about it. And you're not firing questions at me any more.'

'Perhaps I've had my fill for now.'

'Right. Okay,' she said.

He couldn't dismiss the hurt he heard in her voice. Turning, he watched her slim fingers play with the sugary white sand next to her feet. The desire to have those hands on his body grew until it became a physical pain.

Abruptly, he leaned forward and opened the gourmet picnic basket that had been delivered by his crew. He bypassed the food and reached for the chilled champagne. Popping the cork, he poured a glass and handed it to her.

'What are we celebrating?'

'The end of our beautiful down time. We leave for New York in the morning.'

Her eyes widened. Hell, he was more shocked than she was. His plan had been to stay for a full week. But the restlessness that had pounded through him all day wouldn't abate and he needed to find some perspective before it was too late.

At least once they returned to New York, back into the swing of things, everything would make sense again.

'You've asked my every thought for the last six hours. I think it's my turn now.'

He thought of sparing her the chaos running through his head. Then he mentally shrugged. 'I'm thinking why the thought of being free of you gives me no satisfaction.'

'Wow, you really know how to make a woman feel special, don't you?'

'I don't believe in sugar-coating words.'

'Please, spare me the macho stance. You know how to be gentle. What's going on here, Narciso? Why are you suddenly angry with me?'

He met her cloudy gaze and every thought disappeared but one. 'I'm finding how much I despise the thought of you ever taking another lover.'

Shocked blue eyes darted back to his. 'Narciso—'

'Now I've felt you shatter in my arms, the thought of you with another man makes my head want to explode.'

She gasped. 'Did you really just say that?'

He gave a harsh laugh and shook his head, as if testing his own sanity. '*Sì*, I just did.'

Beautifully curved eyebrows rose. 'And I'm guessing that's the first time you've admitted that to a woman?'

'It's the first time I've *felt* that way about any woman.' He shoved a hand through his hair.

Dio mio, he was like a leaking tap! Yesterday, he'd bared his past and his soul as if he were under the influence of a truth serum; today he was contemplating the future and the ache of not having Ruby Trevelli in it.

He knocked back the rest of his drink and surged to his feet. The crew member manning the launch a few dozen metres away looked his way and Narciso beckoned him over.

'It's time to go.' Reality and the cut and thrust of Wall Street would bring some much-needed common sense.

Unlike when they'd donned their swimming gear and laughingly dived from the side of the boat half an hour ago, silence reigned on the way back to *The Warlock.*

When he helped her up from the launch onto the floating swim deck at the back of the yacht, he forced himself to let her go, to stop his hands from lingering on her skin. As much as he wanted to touch her, weave his fingers through the damp hair curling over her shoulders, he couldn't give in to the spell threatening to pull him under.

'I have work to do. I'll catch up with you later.' With his insides twisting into seething knots, he walked away.

Ruby watched him walking away, a giant chasm opening up where pleasure had been half an hour ago. Things had been perfect. So much so, she'd pinched herself a couple of times to make sure the combination of sun, sea and drop-dead-gorgeous companion who'd laughed at her jokes and insisted on knowing every thought in her head was real.

She hadn't told him every thought, of course. For instance, she hadn't admitted that every time he'd touched her she'd heard angels sing to her soul. *That* would've been nuts. As would've been the admission that she was dying to make love with him again.

No chance of that now...

The hard-assed, enigmatic Narciso Valentino of three days ago hadn't made a comeback—and Ruby hoped against all hope the Narciso who chose to smother away his pain was gone for good—but a new Narciso had taken his place. One who fully recognised his vulnerabilities but then ignored them.

The need to go after him was so strong, she locked her knees and gripped the steel banister. He needed time.

Heck, *she* needed time to grapple with the mass of chaotic emotions coursing through her.

Scrambling for control, she went into her cabin and showered off the seawater. Clad in a long, flowered dress with a long slit down one side, she returned to the bar and lined bottles on the counter. Work would take her mind off her unsettling thoughts about Narciso Valentino.

She was measuring a shot of tequila into a shaker when one of the crew members approached.

'Can I get miss anything to eat?'

She shook her head. He smiled and turned to leave. 'Wait.' He paused. 'Have you seen my phone? I've been looking for it everywhere.'

He smiled. 'Oh, yes. One of my colleagues found it in the kitchen yesterday and handed it to Mr Valentino.'

Narciso had her phone? 'Thank you,' she murmured. She slowly screwed the top back on the bottle she'd opened and put the lemon wedges back in the cooler. Wiping her hands on a napkin, she left the deck.

His study was on the second level, past a large room with a sunken sitting area perfect for a dinner party. Like the rest of the vessel, every nook and cranny screamed bespoke and breathtaking luxury.

He growled admittance after her tense knock.

Seated in a leather armchair behind a large antique desk, he watched her enter with a frown. 'Is something wrong?'

'As long as you can adequately explain why you've commandeered my phone, no.'

'You're expecting a call?' he asked.

'Whether I am or not is beside the point.' She shut the door and approached his desk. 'You've had it since yesterday. Why didn't you hand it over?'

He shrugged. 'It must have slipped my mind.'

Somehow she doubted that. But watching him, seeing his face set in those stern, bleak lines she'd recognised from before made her heart stutter. She'd seen that look before.

She stepped closer, looked down and saw the pictures and papers strewn on his desk. The date stamp on the nearest one— showing that very morning—made ice slide down her spine. 'This is the business you had to take care of?'

He slowly set down the document in his hand. 'No. Believe it or not, I intended to scrap all this.'

'But?'

'But something came up.'

She glanced down at the photos. All depicted Giacomo. In one of them, the one Narciso had just dropped, he was dining with a stunning woman in her late twenties.

'Is that the *something*?' she asked, telling herself the pain lancing her chest wasn't jealousy.

His mouth tightened. 'We're not having this conversation, Ruby.'

'What happened to the man who was going to try to find a better way than this need to destroy and annihilate?'

His head tilted. 'That means the same thing.'

'Excuse me?'

'Destroy and annihilate—same meaning.'

'Really? That's all you have to contribute to this conversation?'

His jaw tightened. 'I told you I was good at adapting, *cara*. So why are you surprised that I'm adapting to the situation I find myself in? And seriously, screwing my brains out does not entitle you to weigh in on this.' He waved to his desk.

'Then why did you share it with me?' she replied.

For a moment he floundered. The clear vulnerability in his eyes made her breath catch. 'A misjudgment on my part.'

'I don't believe you.'

Shock widened his eyes. It occurred to her that she was probably the only person who'd dared challenge him this way.

Slowly, his face transformed into an inscrutable mask. Hell, he was so expert at hiding his feelings, he didn't need a mask at his next ball, she thought vaguely.

'I don't care whether you believe me or not. All I care about, what *you* should care about, is whether you can deliver on our agreement. I can easily find a replacement for you if you wish to terminate it when we get back to New York. Believe that.'

'Oh, I believe you. I also believe you think you can hide behind hatred and revenge to find the closeness you seek.'

'*Madre di Dio.* When I suggested you tell me every thought that came into your head, I had no idea you were a closet pop psychologist or I'd have thought twice. I unequivocally revoke that request, by the way.'

Listening to him denigrate what had been a perfect few hours in her life made anger and pain rock through her. Stepping back from the desk, she glanced at the picture, pain slashing her insides.

'I'll leave you to your machinations.' She rushed out and hurried up the stairs, swiping at the foolish tears clouding her vision.

If Narciso wanted to bury himself in the past, he was welcome to do so.

CHAPTER TEN

'THERE'S A NEW recipe I want to try. Care to join me?'

Ruby looked up as Michel approached the counter she'd been working at for the last two hours.

Her mood had vacillated between anger and hurt, undecided on which emotion had the upper hand. Certainly, the piece of meat she'd been hammering was plenty tenderised.

She set it to one side, went to the sink to wash her hands, and rested her hip against the granite trim. 'As long as it's nothing Sicilian. I've had my fill of Sicilians for the foreseeable future.'

Michel cast her a curious glance, then gave a sly smile. 'No, what I'm thinking of is unapologetically French.'

She wiped her hand on her apron. 'Then count me in.'

'Excellent! It's a *sauce au chocolat* with a twist. You're making *croquembouche* for monsieur's dinner party in New York, *oui?*'

'Yes.' Although right now the thought of monsieur himself sautéed in a hot sizzling pan sounded equally satisfying.

'*Bien,* I thought instead of the caramel you could try using chillies.'

'Chilli chocolate? I love the idea. I always convince myself the heat burns away half the calories.'

He gave a very Gallic shrug. 'In my opinion, you do not need to worry about calories, *'moiselle.*'

The compliment took her by surprise. 'Umm, thanks, Michel.'

He shrugged again and started grabbing ingredients off the

shelves. They worked in harmony, measuring, chopping, straining until the scent of the rich chocolate sauce bubbling away in the pan filled the kitchen.

On a whim, she asked, 'Do you have any fresh vanilla pods? I want to try something.'

He nodded. Opening his spice cabinet, he grabbed the one long pod and handed it to her. Ruby cut it open and scraped out the innards. Then, slicing a few strips, she dropped them into the sauce. 'Let that infuse for a few minutes, and we'll try it.'

He rubbed his hands together with a childlike glee that made her laugh. After two minutes he grabbed a clean spoon and scooped a drop of the sauce. 'As the last ingredient was your idea, you sample it first.' He blew on it and held it to her lips.

She tasted it, shut her eyes to better feel the flavours exploding on her tongue. The decadent taste made her groan long and deeply.

'Ruby.'

Her name was a crack of thunder that had her spinning round.

Narciso stood in the doorway, the look on his face as dark and stormy as the tension thickening the air. For several seconds, everyone remained frozen.

Then silver eyes flicked to the Frenchman. 'Leave.'

Michel's eyes widened at the stark dismissal. Narciso took a single step forward to allow the chef to sidle past before he slammed the door shut behind him.

The sound of the lock turning made her nerves scream.

Slowly, Narciso walked towards her. With his every step she willed her feet to move in the other direction, away from the imposing body and icy fury bearing down on her. But she remained frozen.

She held her breath as he stopped a whisper from her.

'My intention was to find you and explain things better, perhaps even apologise for what I said in my study.'

Her heart lifted, then plummeted again when she deciphered his meaning. 'Well, I'm waiting.'

'Oh, you won't be getting an apology from me *now, amante.*'

He leaned over and looked into the copper pan bubbling on the stove. Picking up a spoon, he scooped up some sauce and sampled it.

'Not half bad. What is it?'

'Oh, I thought you'd recognise it, Narciso. This sauce I've named The Valentino Slimeball Special. It'll taste divine with the freshly made Playboy's Puffballs I'm planning on serving them with. You'll love it, trust me.'

Slowly, he lowered the spoon and speared her with those icy silver eyes. 'Say that again.'

'I'm pretty certain there's nothing wrong with your hearing.'

He tossed the spoon into the sink and leaned closer, bracing his hands on either side of her so she was locked in. 'Say it again anyway. I like the way that pretty mouth of yours pouts when you say *puffballs*.'

Despite his indolent words, his eyes glinted with fury. Her instinct warned her to retreat, but caged in like this, watching the erratic pulse beating at his throat, she knew any attempt at escape would be futile.

He was hanging on to his control by a thread. The sudden urge to shatter it the way he seemed to shatter hers so very easily made her stand her ground.

'You'll have to beg me if you want that.'

'Ah, Ruby, shall I let you in on personal insight?'

'Can I stop you?'

'I think you delight in pushing my buttons because you know it'll get you kissed. Am I right?'

'You're wrong.'

'Then why are you licking your lips like that? Anticipation has you almost insane with desperation right now.'

'You have a ridiculously high opinion of yourself.'

'Prove me wrong, then.'

'I won't play your stupid games.'

'Scared?'

'No. Uninterested.'

'Believe me, Ruby, this isn't a game.' When his hands went to undo the tie holding her dress together, she batted them away.

'Stop. What's wrong with you?'

His laugh was filled with bitter incredulity. 'I walk in here to find you moaning for another man and you ask *me* what's wrong with me?'

'You're *jealous*?'

Right before her eyes he seemed to deflate. His hold on her dress ties loosened. And the eyes that speared hers held hellish agitation.

'Yes! I'm jealous. Does that make you happy?'

Her senses screamed yes. Jealousy meant that she mattered in some way to him. The way he'd come to matter to her. 'Why did you come in here, Narciso?'

He sucked in a breath. 'I told you, to apologise.'

'Because my feelings are hurt or because *you* hurt me?'

He lifted a hand and trailed his fingers down her cheek. 'Because I hurt you,' he rasped deeply.

The breath shuddered out of her. 'Thank you for that.'

'Don't thank me, Ruby. What I'm feeling...what you make me feel, I don't know what to do with it. It may well come back and bite us both.'

'But at least you're acknowledging it. So what happened in your study?' she asked before she lost her nerve.

His lips firmed. 'That woman in the picture you saw. Her name is Maria.'

She bit her lip to stem the questions flooding her.

'She's Paolina's—my housekeeper's—granddaughter. I met her that summer ten years ago. She came to visit from Palermo. Paolina brought her to the house and we hung out. By the second week I'd convinced her to stay for the whole summer. I believed myself...infatuated with her.' His lips pinched until the skin showed white. 'I was young and naïve and respected her see-but-don't-touch edict. Until I found out she was giving it up to Giacomo.'

Shock rocked through her. 'She was *sleeping* with your father?'

'Not only sleeping with him. He'd convinced her to make a sex tape, which he forced me to watch on the last day of my stay in Sicily.' Something in the way he said it made her tense.

'What do you mean *forced?*'

His teeth bared in a parody of a smile. 'He had two of his bodyguards hold me down in a chair while the video played on a super-wide screen, complete with surround sound. It was quite the cinematic experience.'

Her mouth gaped. '*Oh, my God.* That's vile!'

'That's Giacomo,' he said simply.

'So, what is he doing with her in New York now?'

His jaw clenched. 'I don't know. The reason I opened the file in the first place was to tell my investigator to toss the case.'

'But now you think he's plotting something?'

'She's broke. Which means she's the perfect pawn for Giacomo.'

Ruby wanted to ask him how he knew that, but the forbidding look in his face, coupled with the anguish lurking in his eyes, changed her mind.

With the evidence of the two people who'd betrayed him before him, he'd have to have been a saint to remain unaffected. Hell, the thought of the double blow of betrayal made her heart twist in pain for him.

'I'm sorry I condemned you. I didn't know.'

Mingled fury and anguish battled in his eyes. 'What about this, Ruby *mio?* Do you know *this?*' he muttered roughly.

He parted her dress and his fingers were drifting down the bare skin of her belly, headed straight for her panty line, before she could exhale. Warm, sure fingers slid between her thighs before Ruby knew what had hit her.

Her cry of astonishment quickly morphed into a moan of need as his thumb flicked against her clitoris.

'Narciso!'

'*Dio,* how can I crave you this badly when I didn't know you a week ago?'

Need rammed through her and she clung to him. 'I don't know. You forget that I should hate this, too. I should hate you.'

He leaned in close, until his hot mouth teased her ear lobe. 'But then that would mean you were conforming to some lofty image you have in your head of your ideal man. You'd be denying that our little tiffs make you so wet you can barely stand it. I turn you on. I heat up your blood and make you feel more alive than you've ever felt. I make you crave all the things you've denied yourself. I know this because it's what you make me feel too. Close your eyes, Ruby.'

'No.' But already her eyelashes were fluttering down, heavy with the drugging desire stealing over her.

The next moment, his breath whispered along her jaw. 'Do you want me to stop?'

She groaned. 'Narciso…'

'Say no and I'll end this.'

She whimpered. 'You're not being fair.'

He laughed again. 'No, I'm not, but I never claimed I was a fair man. And when I feel as if my world is unravelling, halos don't sit well on my head.'

His fingers worked faster, firing up sparks of delight in her that quickly flared into flames.

'Oh! Oh, God.'

He kissed her hard and deep, then nibbled the corner of her mouth as she shattered completely. He ran his free hand down her back in a roughly soothing gesture as she floated back down. The mouth at her ear lobe feathered kisses down her jaw to her throat, then back up again.

'I'm sorry that I hurt you, Ruby. But I'm not sorry that I make you feel like this.'

The New York she'd left just days ago to travel to Macau was the same. Ruby knew that, and yet it was as though she were seeing it for the first time.

As they travelled through midtown towards Narciso's penthouse on the Upper East Side, the sights and sounds appeared more vibrant, soulful.

Part of her knew it was because she was seeing it through different eyes. The eyes of a woman who'd been introduced to passion and intense emotion.

She wanted to push that woman far away, deny all knowledge that she existed. But self-delusion had never been her flaw.

She'd slept for most of the four-hour flight from Belize City, a fact for which she was thankful. Awake and in close proximity to Narciso, she didn't think she could've avoided letting him see her confusion.

Their intense encounter in the kitchen on his yacht had been highly illuminating. Very quickly after granting her most delicious release, he'd walked away, leaving her replete and alarmingly teary.

She'd stood in the kitchen long after he'd left, clutching the sink and fighting a need to run after him and offer him comfort.

But how could she have when his words echoed in her ears.

I hurt you…I'm sorry…I crave you…

With each word, her heart had cracked open wider, until she'd been as raw as his voice had been.

As raw as she was now…

The need to run from her thoughts was very tempting. Giving in, she activated her returned phone. Several voice and text messages flooded into her inbox.

Three were from the same number. One she didn't recognise but suspected its origin.

She answered Annie's query as to when she would be returning and declined her invitation to a girls' night out when she was back from the West Coast. She wasn't ready to face anyone yet, least of all her perceptive roommate, when her emotions felt as if they'd been through a shredder.

The second message was from her mother, asking her to get in touch. She tensed as she listened to the message again. On the surface, it sounded innocuous, a mother asking after her child.

But she heard the undercurrents in her mother's voice and the hairs on her neck stood up. The other messages forgotten, she played the message a third time.

'What's wrong?' Narciso's deep voice cut across her flailing emotions.

'Nothing.'

'Ruby.'

She glanced at him, and her heart lurched. 'Don't look at me like that.'

'Like what?'

'Like you care.'

'I care,' he stated simply.

She sucked in a breath. 'How can you? You told me there was nothing beneath the surface, remember?'

She knew she was probably overreacting but the thought that her mother was reaching out to her because her father had in all likelihood had another affair made her stomach clench in anger and despair.

But unlike the numerous times before when she'd been angry with her parent, Ruby was realising just how harshly she'd misjudged her mother.

From the cocoon of self-righteousness, it'd been easy to judge, to see things in black and white. But having experienced how easy it was to lose control beneath the charisma and magnetism of a powerful man, how could she judge her mother?

Sure, she was aware that part of the reason her mother had stuck around was because she craved the fame that came with being part of a power couple. But Ruby also knew, deep down, her mother could be a success on her own.

A strong, warm hand curled over hers. Her gaze flew up to collide with silver eyes. 'I know what I said but I want to know what's going on anyway.'

His concern burrowed deep and found root in her heart. 'My mother left me a message to call her.'

He nodded. 'And this is troubling?'

'Yes. Normally she emails. She only calls me when something...bad happens.'

'Define bad.'

'My father...sleeping with a sous chef, or a waitress, or a member of their filming crew. That kind of *bad*.'

He swore. 'And she calls you to unburden?'

'And to put pressure on me to join their show. She seems to think my presence will curb my father's wandering eyes.'

His gaze remained steady on hers. 'You don't seem angry about it any more.'

Because he'd made her see herself in a different light: one that didn't fill her with bitterness.

Warmth from his hand seeped through, offering comfort she knew was only temporary.

'I've come to accept that sometimes we make choices in the hope that things will turn out okay. We take a leap of faith and stand by our choices. My mother's living in hope. I can't hate her for that.'

A flash of discomfort altered his expression. 'How very accommodating of you.'

'Accommodating? Hardly. Maybe I'm just worn out. Or maybe I'm finally putting myself into someone else's shoes and seeing things from their point of view.'

'And your father?'

'I can't forgive any man who toys with my...a woman's feelings. Who exploits her vulnerabilities and uses them against her.'

His sharp glance told her the barb had hit home. 'If you're referring to what happened in the kitchen—'

'I'm not.' A lance speared her heart. 'I think it's best we forget about that, don't you?'

I think it's best we forget...

He had no idea why that statement twisted in his gut but it did long after they'd reached his underground car park and entered the lift to his penthouse. Beside him Ruby stood stiffly, her face turned away from him.

He'd expected her to protest when he'd demanded she stay with him until after his VIP dinner party.

Instead, she'd agreed immediately.

The idea that she couldn't be bothered to argue with him made another layer of irrational anxiety spike through him.

Roughly he pushed the feeling away, meshed his fingers with Ruby's and tugged her after him when the lift doors opened.

Paolina exited one of the many hallways of his duplex penthouse to greet him.

Despite being in her late sixties, his housekeeper was as sprightly as she'd been when he was a boy.

'Ciao, bambino. Come stai?'

He responded to the affectionate greeting, let himself be kissed on both cheeks; allowed himself to bask in the warmth of her affection. But only for a second.

Catching Ruby to his side, he introduced her, noting her surprise as he mentioned Paolina's name.

She turned to him as Paolina took control of their luggage and headed to the bedrooms. 'Would this be the same Paolina who's related to Maria?'

His smile felt tight. *'Sì.'*

'I...I thought...'

'That I was a complete monster who cut everyone out of my life because of one incident? I'm not a complete bastard, Ruby.'

'No, you're not,' she murmured.

Her smile held none of the vivacity he'd come to expect. To *crave*. He wanted to win that smile back. Wanted to share what plans he'd put in place before they left Belize. But unfamiliar fear held him back.

Would she judge him for doing too little too late?

He watched her turn a full circle in the large living room, her gaze taking in and dismissing the highly sought-after pieces of art and exclusive decorative accessories most guests tended to gush over. The location of his apartment alone—on a thirtieth floor overlooking Central Park—was enough to pull a strong reaction from even the most jaded guest.

Ruby seemed more interested in the doors leading out of the room. 'Do you mind showing me to the kitchen? I'd like to see where I'll be working and if there's any equipment I need to hire. I should also have the final menu for you shortly. If there's anything you need to change I'd appreciate it if you let me know ASAP.'

Again he felt that unsettled notion of unravelling control. But then…when it came to Ruby, had he held control in the first place?

It certainly hadn't felt like it when he'd walked in on Ruby and Michel. Hearing her moan like that had been a stiletto wound to his heart.

In his jealousy and blind fury had he taken things too far? He tried to catch her eye as he walked beside her towards the kitchen but she refused to look at him.

He'd never had a problem with being given the silent treatment. But right now he wanted Ruby to speak, to tell him what was on her mind.

'What I've seen so far of the menu's fine. It's the perfect blend of continental Europe and good old-fashioned Italian. The guests will appreciate it.'

Her only reaction was to nod. They reached the kitchen and she moved away from him.

She inspected the room with a thoroughness that spoke of a love for her profession. Her long, elegant fingers ran over appliances and worktops and he found his disgruntlement escalating.

Dio, was he really so pathetic as to be jealous of stainless-steel gadgets now? He shook his head and stepped back. 'I'm leaving for the office. We will speak this evening.'

Four hours later, he was pacing his office just as he had been last week.

Only this time there was no sign of the ennui that had

gripped him. Instead, a different form of restlessness prowled through him, one that was unfamiliar and mildly terrifying.

He laughed mirthlessly and pushed a hand through his hair. Narciso wasn't afraid to admit so far he wasn't loving being thirty. He seemed to be questioning his every action. He was even stalling on the deal with Vladimir Rudenko. Did he really need to start another media empire in Russia?

Going ahead with it would mean he'd have to spend time in Moscow. Away from New York. Away from Ruby. *Dio,* what the hell was she doing in his head?

Gritting his teeth, he strode to his desk and pressed the intercom that summoned his driver.

The journey from Wall Street to his penthouse took less than twenty minutes but it felt like a lifetime. Slamming the front door, he strode straight into the kitchen. He needed to tell her of his plans. Needed her to know he'd chosen a different path…

She was elbow deep in some sort of mixture. She glanced up, eyes wide with surprise. 'You're back.'

'We need to talk.'

'What about?'

'About Giacomo—' he tensed, then continued '—about my father.'

Her eyes grew wider. 'Yes?'

'I've decided to end—'

A phone beeped on the counter. A look of unease slid over her features as she wiped her hands and activated the message. A few seconds later, all trace of colour left her cheeks. 'I have to go.'

He frowned. 'Go where?'

'Midtown. I'll be back in an hour.'

'I'll drive you—'

'No. I'll be fine. Really. I've been cooped up in here all afternoon. I need the fresh air.'

'Fresh air in New York is a misnomer.' He continued to watch her, noting her edginess. 'Is it your parents?'

Her fingers twisted together. 'No, it's not.' Sincerity shone from her eyes.

He nodded. 'Fine. I just wanted you to know, you have my backing one hundred per cent. After the party, I'll have the papers drawn up to provide the funds you need for the restaurant.'

'Th-thank you. That's good news.' The definite lack of pleasure on her face and voice caused his spine to stiffen. She reached him and tried to slide past.

Unable to help himself, he caught her to him and kissed her soft, tempting mouth. She yielded to the kiss for a single moment before she wrenched herself away.

'Amante—'

'I have to go.'

Before he could say another word she snatched her bag from the counter and walked out of the door.

Narciso stood frozen, unable to believe what had happened. By the time he forced himself to move, Ruby was gone.

CHAPTER ELEVEN

RUBY ENTERED THE upscale restaurant at the stroke of six and gave her name.

A waiter ushered her to a window seat. It took seconds to recognise the man at the table. Shock held her rigid as she stared at him.

Without his mask, Giacomo Valentino bore a striking resemblance to his son. Except his eyes were dull with age and his mouth cruel with entrenched bitterness.

'I knew I recognised you from somewhere, Ruby Trevelli,' Giacomo Valentino said the moment she sat down. 'The wonders of modern technology never cease to amaze me. A few clicks and I had everything I needed to know about you and your parents.'

She tensed. 'What do you want?'

'A way to bring my son down. And you will help me.'

She rushed to her feet. 'You're out of your mind.'

'I met with your loan shark today,' he continued conversationally. 'As of three hours ago, I own twenty-five per cent of your yet-to-be-built restaurant. If you walk out of here, I'll call in the debt immediately.'

Heart in her throat, she slowly sank back into her seat. 'Why are you doing this?'

His face hardened. 'You saw how he humiliated me in Macau.'

'Yes, and since then I've also heard what you did to him. And I know you met with Maria yesterday.'

A flash of fear crossed his face but it was quickly smothered. 'So Narciso knows?'

'Yes.'

The old man visibly paled.

'Give it up, Giacomo. You're out of options because there's no way I'll help you further your vendetta against your own flesh and blood.'

The flash came again, and this time she saw what it was. Deep, dark, twisted pain. 'He's a part of me that should never have come into being.'

She shook her head. 'How can you say that?'

'He took away from me the one thing I treasured most in this world. And he struts around like the world owes him a living.'

Ruby heard the black pain behind his words and finally understood. Deep down, Giacomo Valentino was completely and utterly heartbroken over losing his wife.

A part of her felt sympathy for him. But she could tell Giacomo was too set in his thinking to alter his feelings towards his son.

Narciso, on the other hand, wasn't. Ruby had seen gentleness in him. She'd seen compassion, consideration, even affection towards Paolina, the grandmother of the woman who'd betrayed him. He had the capacity to love, if only he'd step back from the brink of the abyss of revenge he was poised on.

And will you be the one to save him?

Why not? He'd helped her come to terms with her own relationship with her parents. She'd called her mother this afternoon, and, sure enough, her father had strayed again. But this time, Ruby had offered her mother a shoulder to cry on. They'd spoken for over an hour. Tears had been shed on both sides. An hour later, she'd received a text from her mother to say she'd contacted an attorney and filed for a divorce from her husband.

Ruby knew the strength it'd taken for her mother to break free. Taking a deep breath, she looked Giacomo in the eye. 'You probably don't want my advice but I'll give it anyway. You and Narciso both lost someone dear to you. You were lucky enough to know her. Have you spared a thought for the child who never knew his mother?'

'*Ascolta—!*'

'No, you listen. Punishing a baby for its mother's death went out with the Dark Ages. Do you have any idea how much he's hurting?'

Pale silver eyes narrowed. 'You're in love with my son.'

Her heart lurched, then hammered as if fighting to get away from the truth staring her in the face. Her fingers tightened on her bag. 'I won't be a party to whatever you're cooking up.'

'You disappoint me, Miss Trevelli. Before you go, I should tell you that your loan shark provided me with an extensive file on you, which details, among other things, a building on Third and Lexington.'

Panic flared high. '*My parents' restaurant?*'

Giacomo gave a careless nod.

'I swear, if you dare harm them I'll—'

Giacomo put a hand on her arm. 'My request is simple.'

She wanted to bolt but she remained seated.

His speculative gaze rested on her. 'My son is taken with you. More than he has been with any other woman.'

Her insides clenched hard. 'You're wrong—'

'I'm right.' He leaned forward suddenly. 'I want you to end your relationship with him.'

Her mouth dried. 'There is no relationship.'

'End it. Sever all ties with him and I'll make sure your parents' livelihood remains intact. I'll even become your benefactor with your restaurant.'

Frantically she shook her head. 'I don't want your charity.'

His eyes narrowed. 'Do you really want to risk crossing me? I urge you to remember where my son inherited his thirst for revenge from.'

Feeling numb, she rose. This time he didn't stop her.

Her thin sweater did nothing to hold the April chill at bay

as she blindly struck through the evening crowd. She only realised where she was headed when the subway train pulled into
the familiar station.

Her apartment was soothingly quiet. Dropping her bag, she
went to the small bar she'd installed when she moved in.

Blanking her thoughts, she went to work, mixing liqueurs
with juices, spirits with the bottle of champagne she'd been
gifted on her birthday. Carefully she lined up the mixtures that
worked and discarded the rest. She was on her last set when she
heard the pounding on the door.

Breath catching, she went to the door and glanced into the
peeper.

Narciso loomed large and imposing outside her door. Jumping back, she toyed with not answering.

'Let me in, Ruby. Or so help me, I'll break this door down.'

With shaking hands, she released the latch.

He took a single, lunging step in and slammed the door behind him. 'You said you'd be an hour, tops.' Silver eyes bore
into her, intense and frighteningly invasive.

She forced a shrug. 'I lost track of time.'

'If you wanted to return here all you needed was to say.'
There was concern in his voice, coupled with the vulnerability
he'd been unable to hide on the yacht.

Knowing what had put that vulnerability there, knowing
what his father's lack of love had done to him, made her chest
tighten. She so desperately wanted to reach for him, to soothe
his pain away.

But in light of what she faced, there was only one recourse
where Narciso was concerned. 'I didn't realise I had to answer
to you for my movements.'

He frowned and speared a hand through his hair. The way
it fell made her guess he'd been doing it for a while. Swallow-
ing hard, she forced her gaze away and walked into the small
living room.

He followed. 'You don't,' he answered. 'But you said you'd
come back. And you didn't.'

'It's no big deal, Narciso. I wanted to return home for a bit.'

'Are you ready to return now?' he shot back, his gaze probing.

The need to say yes sliced through her. 'No. I think I'll spend the night here.'

He started to speak. Stopped, and looked around. She didn't even bother to look at her apartment through his eyes. Annie had used the term shabby chic when they'd picked up knick-knacks from flea markets and second-hand shops to furnish their apartment. The plump sofas were mismatched, as were the lamps and cushions. The pictures that hung on the walls were from sidewalk artists whose talent had caught Ruby's eye.

'Why are you here, Narciso?'

Narciso walked over to a lampshade and touched the bohemian fringe. 'I tried to tell you earlier. I've called off the vendetta with my father.'

Shock rocked through her, followed swiftly by sharp regret. 'Why?'

He shoved his hand into his pockets and inhaled. 'In a word? *You*. You're the reason.' Again that vulnerability blazed from his eyes. Along with a wariness as she remained frozen.

'I shouldn't be the reason, Narciso. You should do it for yourself.'

He shrugged. 'I'm working my way to that, *amante*. But I need your help. You set me on this road. You can't walk away now.'

Oh, God!

She choked back a sob and fled to the bar. He followed and saw the drinks lined up on the counter.

'You were working?'

'I never stop.'

'What have you come up with?' There was a genuine interest in his tone. For whatever reason, he wanted to know more about her passion.

His softening attitude towards her sent her emotions into panicked freefall. Belize had warned her she was at serious risk of developing feelings for Narciso Valentino. Seeing him in her home, touching her things, making monumental confessions, made her want to rush to him and burrow into his chest, hear his heart pounding against her own. But she couldn't. Not now.

She shoved her hands into her jeans pockets and shrugged. 'This and that.'

He flicked a glance at her. Then he picked up the nearest drink and took a sip. 'What's this one called?'

Push him away!

She took a deep, frantic breath. '*Sleazy Playboy*. The one next to it is *The Studly Warlock*, the blue one is the *Belize Bender*, and the pink one I've termed *The Virgin Sacrifice*.'

He stiffened.

'There's a black Sambuca one I'm intending to call *Crazy, Stupid Revenge*—'

'Enough, Ruby. I get the message. I've upset you. Again. Tell me how to make it better.' He looked over at her and his eyes held a simple, honest plea.

Dear God. Narciso wasn't all gone at all. In fact, right at that moment, he was the single, most appealing thing in her life.

Heat and need and panic and lust surged under her skin as his gaze remained steady on hers. With every fibre in her being she wanted to cross the room and launch herself into his arms.

Giacomo's face flashed across her mind.

'There's nothing to make better because there's nothing between us.'

His eyes widened. *'Scusi?'*

'We had what we had, Narciso. Let's not prolong it any further.'

His eyes slowly hardened. In quick strides, he crossed the room and jerked her into his body. The contact threatened to sizzle her brain. Throwing out her hands against his chest, she tried to break free. He held tight.

'Let me go!'

'Why? Scared I'll prove you wrong?'

'Not at all—'

He swooped down and captured her mouth. His kiss was raw, possessive and needy.

'What the hell's happening, Ruby?' he whispered raggedly against her mouth.

Again her heart skittered.

Briefly, she thought to come clean, tell him where she'd been. Panic won out.

'Dammit, Ruby, kiss me back!' he pleaded raggedly against her lips.

She couldn't deny him any more than she could deny herself what would surely be her last time of experiencing this magic with him.

Desperate hands grazed over his chest to his taut stomach. Grasping the bottom of his T-shirt, she pulled it up. He helped her by tugging it over his head and flinging it away. Eyes blazing with an emotion she was too afraid to name met hers. Stepping forward, she placed an open-mouthed kiss on his collarbone.

His hiss of arousal echoed around the room. Emboldened, she used her teeth, tongue and mouth to drive them both crazy. When he stumbled slightly, she realised she'd pushed him towards the sofa. With a hard push she sent him sprawling backwards. Within seconds he was naked, his perfect body beckoning irresistibly. Driven by guilt and hunger, she stripped off her T-shirt and bra and unsnapped her jeans.

With a shake of his head, he covered her hands with his. 'Let me.'

The slow slide downward was accompanied by hot, worshipful kisses that brought tears to her eyes. Afraid her emotions would give her away, she hurriedly stepped out of the jeans and pushed him back down again and resumed the path she'd charted moments before.

His groan when her lips touched the tip of his shaft was ragged and raw. But encouraging hands speared through her hair, holding her to her task.

Boldly, she took him in her mouth. '*Dio*, Ruby!'

She looked up at him. His eyes were closed, his neck muscles taut from holding on to his control. Taking him deeper, she lost herself in the newfound power and pleasure, her heart singing with an almost frightening joy at being able to do this, one last time.

Tomorrow would bring its own heartache but for now—

'*Basta!*' he rasped. 'As much as I'd love to finish in your mouth, my need to be inside you is even greater.'

He pulled her up and astride him. Reaching for his discarded jeans, he took a condom from his back pocket.

The thought that he'd come prepared dimmed her pleasure for a second. But realising what the alternative would've meant, she took the condom from him, tore it open and slipped it on his thick shaft, experiencing a momentary pang at how big he was.

Silver eyes gleamed at her. 'We fit together perfectly, *tesoro,* remember?' he encouraged gently.

Nodding, she raised her hips and took him inside her.

Delicious, sensational pleasure built inside her, setting off fireworks in her body. His face a taut mask of pleasure, his hands settled on her thighs and he allowed her to set the pace. But this new, deeper penetration was her undoing. Within minutes, her spine tingled with impending climax. She had no resistance when Narciso reared up, sucked one nipple into his mouth and sent her over the edge.

She surfaced from the most blissful release to find their positions reversed. Narciso's fingers were tangled in her hair and his mouth buried in her throat.

When he raised his head, the depth of emotion on his face made her breath catch.

'I need you, Ruby,' he repeated his earlier statement. Only this time, she was sure he didn't mean sexually.

The knowledge that things would never be right between them sent pure, white-hot pain through her heart.

Unable to find the right words to respond, she cradled his face. Locked in that position, his eyes not leaving hers, he surged inside her and resumed the exquisite, soul-searing love-making. Eventually, he groaned his release and took her mouth in a soft, gentle kiss, murmuring words she understood but refused to allow into her heart.

Tears sprang into her eyes and she rapidly blinked them away, glad that he was rising and putting his clothes back on.

'I can stay here, or we can return to my place.' Although his tone wasn't as forceful as before, she knew he wouldn't accept a third choice.

'I'll come back with you.' Despite all that had happened, she still had his dinner party to cater for.

They dressed in silence and she studiously avoided the puzzled glances he sent her way.

When he caught her hand in his in the lift on the way to the ground floor, she let him. When he brought the back of her hand to his lips and kissed it, she sucked in a deep breath to stop the tears clogging her throat from suffocating her.

In his car, he pulled her close, clamped both arms around her and tucked her head beneath his chin. In the long drive back to the Upper East side, neither of them spoke but he took every opportunity to run gentle hands down her arms and over her hair.

Unable to stop herself, she felt tears slide down her cheeks.

Dear God, what the hell had she done? Of all the foolish decisions she could've made, she'd gone and fallen in love with Narciso Valentino.

'Qualunque cosa che, oi facevo io sono spiacente,' he murmured raggedly in her ear. *Whatever I did, I'm sorry.*

The tears fell harder, silent guilty sobs racking her frame.

He led her to the shower the moment they returned to his penthouse. Again, in silence, he washed her, then pulled a clean T-shirt of his over her head. Pulling back the covers to his bed, he tugged her close and turned out the lights.

'We'll talk in the morning, Ruby. Whatever is happening between us, we'll work it out, *si?*'

She nodded, closed her eyes and drifted off to a troubled sleep.

She jerked awake just after 5:00 a.m., fear and anguish

churning through her body. The need to tell Narciso the truth burned through her.

She needed to tell him about the meeting last night. Needed to let him know that Giacomo's thirst for revenge burned brighter than ever.

Her fear for her parents had blinded her to the fact that she was stronger than Giacomo's blackmail threats. There was no way Ruby would do as Giacomo asked.

She loved Narciso, and, if there was any way he reciprocated those feelings, she didn't intend to walk away.

But she had to warn him that Giacomo might come at him by a different means once he found out Ruby had no intention of walking away.

Turning her head, she watched Narciso's peaceful profile as he slept. Her heart squeezed and she sucked in a breath as tears threatened.

She'd never have believed she could fall in love so quickly and so deeply. But in less than a week she'd fallen for the world's number-one playboy.

But there was far more to Narciso than that. And if there was a chance for them...

Vowing to speak to him after the party, she slid out of bed, dressed without waking him and left the bedroom.

Armed with the black card he'd given her yesterday, she went outside and hailed a taxi. The market in Greenwich was bustling by the time she arrived just before six. For the next hour, she lost herself in picking the freshest vegetables, fruit and staples she needed for the dinner party.

Next, she stopped at the upmarket wine stockist.

Narciso had enough wine and vintage champagne so she only selected the spirits and liqueurs she needed for her cocktails.

She was leaving the shop when her phone buzzed. Heart jumping into her throat because she knew who it would be, she answered.

'You left without waking me,' came the quiet accusation.

'I needed to get to the market before sunrise.'

He sighed. 'I'm sorely tempted to cancel this event but I have several guests flying in specially.'

'Why would you want to cancel it?'

'Because it's coming between me and what I want right now.'

Her heart thundered. 'Wh-what do you want?'

'You. Alone. A proper conversation with no disturbances. To get to the bottom of whatever last night was about.'

'I'm sorry, I should've told you…' She stopped as a phone rang in the background.

'*Scusi,*' he excused himself, only to return a minute later. 'I need to head to the office but I'll be back by five tonight, *sì?*'

'Okay, I'll see you then.'

He paused, as if he wanted to say something. Then he ended the call.

Ruby was glad for the distraction of getting everything ready for the dinner party. By the time Michel showed up midafternoon, she'd almost finished her preparations.

They talked through the recipes she'd planned and settled on the timing.

'Monsieur tells me you'll be manning the bar tonight?'

'The idea is to divide my time between the bar and the kitchen. I know I can trust you to hold the fort here?'

'Of course.' He peered closer at her. 'Is everything all right?'

She busied herself placing large chunks of freshly cut salmon in its foil wrappings.

'It will be when the evening's over. I always get the jitters at these events.'

His knowing glance told her he hadn't missed her evasiveness. Thankfully, Paolina entered the kitchen and Ruby sighed with relief.

The planning team arrived at four. After that, deliveries flooded in. Flowers, a DJ and lighting specialists who set up on the terrace.

But the most unexpected delivery came in the form of a couture designer bearing a zipped-up garment bag, which she handed over and promptly departed. The note pinned to the stunning powder-blue floor-length gown was simple—*a beautiful gown for a beautiful woman.*

Joy burst through her heart, made her smile for the first time that day.

For the job she had to do tonight, it was severely impractical, as were the silver shoes almost the exact shade as Narciso's eyes, but as she walked into Narciso's bedroom and hung up the dress she knew she would wear it.

Narciso was late. He arrived barely a half-hour before his guests were due to arrive and walked into the bedroom just as she was putting finishing touches to her upswept hair.

He froze in the doorway, and stared. 'You look gorgeous, *bellissima.*'

She turned from the mirror, a cascade of love, trepidation and anxiety smashing through her. How would he take the news of his father's continued scheming?

Remember where my son inherited his thirst for revenge...

Forcing down the shiver of apprehension, she murmured, *'Grazie.'*

His eyes darkened with pleasure. 'You need to speak more Italian. Or better still Sicilian. I'll teach you,' he said as he shrugged off his jacket and tugged at his tie.

Then he strode to where she stood. Snaking a large hand around her nape, he pulled her in for a long, deep kiss. Then with a groan he stepped back.

'Give me fifteen minutes and I'll be with you.'

'Okay.'

'Dio, I must be growing a conscience, *bellissima,* since I keep dismissing the idea of calling this party off.'

She forced a laugh. 'You must be.'

Shaking his head, he entered the bathroom. She stood there until the sound of the shower pulled her from her troubled thoughts.

She was behind the bar, pouring the first of the cocktails into glasses, when he emerged.

The sight of him in a superbly cut grey suit and a blue shirt that matched her dress made her heart slam into her throat. He'd taken a single step towards her when the doorbell rang.

He rolled his eyes dramatically, then his gaze drifted over her in heated promise before he nodded for the butler to answer the door.

For the next two hours, Ruby let her skills take over, serving food that drew several compliments from the dinner guests.

She declined when Narciso invited her to join them at the dinner table. Although his eyes narrowed in displeasure, there was very little he could do about it, much to her relief.

She was preparing a round of after-dinner cocktails when she looked up and gasped.

Giacomo was framed in the penthouse doorway.

Her gaze swung to Narciso; frozen, she watched his head turn and his body tense as he saw his father.

For several seconds, they eyed each other across the room.

Giacomo sauntered in as if he belonged. Several guests, sensing the altered atmosphere, glanced between father and son.

'Hey, watch it!'

She jerked and looked down to find she'd overfilled a glass and the lime-green cocktail was spilling over the counter.

Setting the shaker down, she grabbed a napkin.

'*Bona sira,* Ruby,' came the mocking voice. 'How lovely you look.'

Her head snapped up and connected with Giacomo's steely gaze. Surprise that he hadn't headed straight for his son held her immobile. Long enough for him to calmly reach across the counter, take her hand and press a kiss on her knuckles.

She tried to snatch her hand away but he held on tight, a triumphant smile playing about his lips. 'Play along, little one, and all your problems will go away,' he said in a low voice.

'I have no intention of playing along with anything.'

'It doesn't matter one way or the other. Narciso is infatuated with you. He'll see what I want him to see.'

With the clarity of a klaxon, everything fell into place.

She'd been played. Giacomo had always intended *this* to be his revenge. By meeting with him last night, she'd only given him more ammunition.

Heart shattering, she glanced over to where Narciso stood stock still, his eyes icy lakes of shock.

CHAPTER TWELVE

'NARCISO—'

'Don't speak.'

Narciso paced in his office, marvelling at how his voice emerged so calm, so collected, when his insides bled from a million poisonous cuts.

'Listen to him, *bedda*. He's prone to childish tantrums when he's upset. Just look at how he threw out all his guests a few minutes ago—'

'Shut up, old man, or so help me I'll bury my fist in your face.'

Giacomo shook his head and glanced at Ruby in a *what-did-I-say?* manner.

'What the hell are you doing here?'

'Ruby told me you were having a party. I decided to invite myself.'

'I didn't—!'

'*Ruby* told you? When?' Narciso's gaze swung to her, then returned to his father.

'Last night, when she met me for dinner.'

'He's lying, Narciso.' He heard the plea in her voice and tried to think, to rationalise what was unfolding before him. Unfortunately his brain seemed to have stopped working.

From the moment he'd seen Giacomo take her hand and kiss it, time had jerked to a stop, then rewound furiously, throwing up old memories that refused to be banished.

Forcing himself into the present, he stared at Ruby. The gorgeous firecracker who'd got under his skin. The woman who'd made love to him last night in her apartment as if her soul belonged to him.

Waking up this morning to find her gone had rocked him to his soul. The realisation that he wanted her in his bed and in his arms every morning and night for the rest of his life had been shocking but slowly, as the idea had embedded itself into his heart, he'd known it was what he wanted.

He loved her. He, who'd never loved anything or anyone in his life, had fallen in love...

With a woman who would meet with his father and not tell him...allow Giacomo to put his hand on her.

No! He couldn't have made the same mistake twice.

Ruby was different...

Wasn't she? Reeling, he watched Giacomo stroll to the large sofa in the room and ease himself into it. His attitude reeked a confidence that shook Narciso to the core.

He forced himself to speak. 'Ruby, is this true?'

She shook her head so emphatically, tendrils fell down her graceful neck. 'No, it's not. I only—'

'You have a spy following me around. I know you do. He reports to you twice a week. Today is one of those days, I believe,' Giacomo said.

Narciso's fists tightened. 'Not any more.'

Surprise lit the old man's eyes. 'Really? You must be going soft. Luckily, I had my own pictures taken.'

Giacomo reached into his pocket and threw down a set of photos on the coffee table.

Narciso felt his body tremble as he moved towards the table. For the first time in his life, he knew genuine fear. He glanced up to see Ruby's eyes on his face.

'Please, Narciso, it's not what you think. I can explain.'

He took another step. And there in Technicolor was the woman he loved, with the man he'd believed until very recently he hated most in his life.

Ironically, it was Ruby who'd made him look deeper into himself and acknowledge the fact that it wasn't hate that drove him but a desperate need to connect with the person who should've loved him.

His legs lost the ability to support him and he sank into his chair. Vicious pain slashed at his heart and he fought against the need to howl in agony.

'Leave,' he rasped.

'I warned you you would never best me,' his father crooned.

Slowly, Narciso raised his head and looked at his father. Despite his triumph, he looked haggard. The years of bitterness had taken their toll. It was what he'd risked becoming...

'She insisted on saving you, do you know that?'

Ice filled his gut. *'Scusi?'*

Giacomo's gaze scoured him. 'Your *mamma*. She had a chance to live. The doctor who arrived could only save one of you. She had a chance and she chose you.' Bitterness coated every word.

'And you've hated me for it ever since, haven't you?'

Giacomo's face hardened. 'I never wanted children. She knew that. If she'd only listened to me, she'd still be alive.' He inhaled and surged to his feet. 'What does it matter? Come, Ruby. You're no longer wanted here.'

Narciso snarled. 'Lay another finger on her and it's the last thing you'll ever do.'

His father jerked in shock, then his face took on a grey hue. Narciso watched, stunned, as Giacomo clutched his chest and began to crumple.

'Narciso, I think he's having a heart attack!'

For several seconds Ruby's words didn't compute. When the meaning spiked, poker hot, into his brain, he reached out and caught Giacomo as he fell.

Behind him he heard Ruby dialling and speaking to emergency personnel as he tore open his father's shirt and began chest compressions.

'Madre di Dio, non,' he whispered, the fear clutching his chest beginning to spread as his father lay still.

The next fifteen minutes passed by in a blur. The ER helicopter landed on the penthouse roof and emergency personnel took over.

He sagged against a wall when they informed him Giacomo was still alive but would need intensive care immediately.

'He'll pull through. I'm sure of it.'

He looked up to find Ruby in front of him, holding out a glass of whisky. He took it and knocked it back in one gulp.

It did nothing to thaw the ice freezing his heart.

'Leave.' He repeated the word he'd said what seemed like a lifetime ago.

Shock rushed over her face.

'Narciso—'

He threw the glass across the room and heard it shatter. 'No. You don't get to say my name. Never again.'

He took satisfaction in seeing tears fill her eyes. 'I can explain—'

'It's too late. I told you this thing between Giacomo and I was over. I'd trusted your counsel, taken your advice and abandoned this godforsaken vendetta. But where was your trust, *tesoro mio*? You knew this was coming. And you said nothing!'

'He threatened my parents!'

His expression softened for a split second. Then grew granite hard. 'Of course he did. But his threats meant more to you than your belief that I would help you. That we could fight him together!' He couldn't hide the raw pain that flowed out of his voice.

'I didn't want to fight! And I was going to tell you. Tonight after the party.'

'We'll never know now, will we?' he said scathingly.

'Narciso—'

'Your actions spoke clearly for you. Unfortunately for you, you made the same mistake Maria did. *You chose the wrong side.*'

* * *

Ruby smoothed her hand down the sea-green dress and tried to stem the butterflies.

In less than half an hour, the grand opening of Dolce Italia would be under way.

Two months of sheer, sometimes blessedly mind-numbing, hard work. She'd volunteered for every job that didn't require specialist training in the blind hope of drowning out the acute pain and devastation of having to live without Narciso. Her success rate had been woefully pathetic...

'Are you ready yet, *bella bambina?* The paparazzi will be here in a minute.' Her mother entered, wearing an orange silk gown that pleasantly complemented her slim figure. Despite being in her late forties, Paloma looked ten years younger. With her divorce from her philandering husband firmly underway, she appeared to have acquired a new lease on life. The spring in her step had grown even bolder when Ruby had allowed her to take a financial stake in the restaurant.

She stopped in the middle of the small room they'd converted to a dressing room at the back of the two-storey restaurant and cocktail bar in the prime location in Manhattan.

'Oh, you look stunning,' she said, then her eyes darkened with worry. 'A little on the thin side, though.'

'Don't fuss, Mamma.'

'It's my job to fuss. A job I neglected for years.'

Knowing she was about to lapse into another self-recriminating rant, Ruby rushed forward and hugged her. 'What's done is done, Mamma. Now we look forward.'

Her mother blinked brown eyes bright with unshed tears and nodded. 'Speaking of moving forward, the most exquisite bouquet of flowers arrived for you.'

Ruby's breath caught, then rushed out in a gush of pain. 'I don't want them.'

Her mother frowned. 'What woman doesn't want flowers on the most spectacular night of her life?'

'Me.'

'Are you sure you're all right? Last week you sent back that superb crate of white Alba truffles, the week before you refused the diamond tennis bracelet. I wish you'd tell me who all these gifts are from.'

'It doesn't matter who they're from. I don't want any of them.' She fought the rising emotions back. She'd shed enough tears to last her a lifetime.

Not tonight. With her mother as her new business partner, she'd paid off Giacomo's loan and closed that chapter.

Tonight, she would push Narciso and his in-your-face gifts out of her mind and bask in her accomplishment.

'I'm ready.'

They entered the large reception area to find a three-deep row of photographers and film crew awaiting them. In the time she'd decided to open the restaurant with her mother, Paloma had guided her in how to deal with the press. Where her reaction to them had been led by fear and resentment, now she used banter and firmness to achieve her aim.

With the press conferences and TV junkets taken care off, her mother passed her the scissors and she moved to a large white ribbon.

'Ladies and gentlemen, my mother, Paloma, and I are proud to declare Dolce Italia open—'

At first she thought she was hallucinating. Then the face became clearer.

Narciso stood to one side of the group, his silver eyes square on her face.

'Ruby?' she heard her mother's concerned voice from far away as the heavy scissors slipped from her grasp.

'Ruby!'

She turned and fled.

'Ruby.' He breathed her name as if it were a life-giving force, pulling her from the murky depth of pain. 'Open the door, *per favore.*'

She snatched the door she'd slammed shut moments ago

wide open. 'You ruined my opening. Weeks of preparation, of breaking my back to make this perfect, and you swooped in with your stupid face and your stupid body and *ruined* it.' She found herself inspecting his face and body and tore her gaze away.

'*Mi dispiace.* I wanted...I *needed* to see you.'

'Why? What could you possibly have to say to me that you haven't already said?'

His jaw tightened. 'A lot. You returned all my gifts.'

'I didn't want them.'

He took a step into the room. 'And the NMC cheque? You returned it to me ripped into a hundred pieces.'

'I was making a point. Why did you keep sending me stuff?'

'Because I refused to contemplate giving up. I refused to imagine what my life would be like without the thinnest thread of hope keeping me going.'

She wanted to keep her gaze averted, but, like a magnet, it swung towards him.

He looked incredible, the five-o'clock shadow gracing his jaw making him look even more stunning. But a closer look pinpointed a few surprising changes.

'You've lost weight,' she murmured.

He shut the door behind him and she caught the faint snick of the lock. 'So have you. At least I have an excuse.'

'Really?'

'*Sì,* Michel threatened to quit. We agreed on a month-long vacation.'

'You don't deserve him.'

He grimaced. 'That's entirely true. He wasn't happy when he realised his culinary efforts were going to waste.' He threaded his fingers together and stared down at them. When he looked back up, his eyes were bleak, infinitely miserable. Her heart kicked hard. 'I can't eat, Ruby. I've barely slept since you left.'

'And this is my fault? I didn't *leave*. You threw me out, re-member?'

He paled and nodded, his nostrils thinning as he sucked in

a long, ragged breath. 'I was wrong. So very wrong to believe even for a second that you were anything like Maria.'

'And you've suddenly arrived at this conclusion?'

'No. All the signs were there. I just refused to see them because I'd programmed myself to believe the worst.'

Her heart kicked again, this time with the smallest surge of hope. 'What signs?'

'Your determination to push me away when I came to your apartment. Your tears in the car on the way back home. Your clear distress when my father touched you. Why would you encourage me to reconcile with my father and turn round and betray me?'

'I wouldn't… I didn't.'

He shook his head. 'I know. I condemned you for something that never happened. Something you tried to tell me you would never do. But I was so bitter and twisted I couldn't see what was in front of me.'

'What was that?'

'The love I have for you and the probability that you could perhaps love me, too.'

Her breath caught. 'W-what?'

'I know I've blown all that now—'

'You mean you don't love me?'

He speared a hand through his hair and jumped up. 'Of course I love you. That's not the point here, I meant—'

'I think you'll find that's the whole point, Narciso,' she murmured, her heart racing.

He stopped. Stared down at her. Slowly his eyes widened. Ruby knew what he was seeing in her face. The love she'd tried for so long and so hard to smother was finally bursting out of her.

'Dio mio,' he breathed.

'You can say that again.'

'Dio mio,' he repeated as he sank onto his knees in front of her. 'Please tell me I'm not dreaming?'

'I love you, Narciso. Despite you being a horrible pain in the ass. There, does that help?'

With a groan, he rose, took her face in his hands and kissed her long and deep. 'I'll dedicate every single moment of the rest of my life to making you forget that incident.'

'That sounds like a great deal.'

'Can I also convince you to let me back Dolce Italia in any way I can?'

Despite the guilt she saw in his face, she shook her head. 'No. It's now a mother-daughter venture. I want to keep it that way.'

'What about your father?' he asked.

'He consults...from afar. We'll never be close but he's my blood. I can't completely cut him off.'

'*Prezioso,* you humble me with how giving you are.'

'You should've remembered that before you pushed me away.'

'I've relived the hell of it every single second since I lost you.'

'Keep telling me that and I may allow you to earn some brownie points.'

He smiled. 'Can we discuss accumulative points?'

'I may be open to suggestions.'

He kissed her until her heart threatened to give out.

'Wow, okay. That could work.'

'How about this, too?'

He reached behind him and presented her with a large leather, velvet-trimmed box. It was far too large to contain a ring but her heart still thundered as she opened it.

The mask was breathtaking. Bronze-trimmed around blue velvet, it was the exact colour of the waters of Belize. Peacock feathers sprouted from the top in a splash of Technicolor, and two lace ties were folded and held down by diamond pins.

'It's beautiful.'

'It's yours if you choose to accompany me on the next *Q Virtus* event.'

'I want to know more about your super-secret club.'

A sly smile curved his lips. 'I could tell you all the secrets, but then I'd have to make love to you for days to make you forget.'

'Hmm, I suppose I'd just have to suffer through it.'

He laughed, pulled her close and kissed her again. She pulled away before things got heavy.

'Tell me what you've done to my mother.'

'She promised to hold the fort on condition I did everything in my power to exit this room as her future son-in-law.'

Ruby gasped. 'She didn't! God, first you muscle in on my opening, then you strike deals behind my back.'

'What can I say? She drives a hard bargain.' He pulled back and stared down at her, a hint of uncertainty in his eyes. 'So will you give me an answer?'

Her arms rose to curl over his shoulders. 'That depends.'

'On what?'

'On whether white Alba truffles come with the deal.'

He pulled her close and squeezed her tight. 'I'll keep you supplied every day for the rest of your life if that's what it takes, *amante*.'

Isla de Margarita, Venezuela

Narciso leaned against the side of the cabana and watched his wife wow the crowd with her latest range of cocktails. Although her mask covered most of her face, he could tell she was smiling.

Music pumped from the speakers strategically placed around the pool area and all around him *Q Virtus* members let their inhibitions fly musically and otherwise.

He raised his specially prepared cocktail to his lips and paused as the lights caught his new wedding ring.

He'd wanted a big wedding for Ruby but she'd insisted on a small, intimate ceremony at the Sicilian villa where he'd been born.

In the end, they'd settled for fifty guests including her

mother, and Nicandro Carvalho and Ryzard Vrbancic, the two men he considered his closest friends.

Although they were working on their relationship, he and Giacomo had a way to go before all the heartache could be set aside.

'So...*last three bachelors standing* becomes two. How the hell are Nicandro and I going to handle all these women by ourselves, huh, my friend?'

Laughing, he turned to Ryzard. 'That's your problem. I'm willingly and utterly taken.' He glanced over and saw Ruby's eyes on him. He raised his glass and winked.

Ryzard shuddered. 'That's almost sickening to watch.'

'If you're going to throw up, do it somewhere else.'

Shaking his head, his friend started to walk away, then Narciso saw him freeze. The woman who had caught his attention was dancing by herself in a corner. Although she had a full mask over her face, her other attributes clearly had an effect on Ryzard.

Smiling, Narciso turned to watch his wife emerge from behind the bar and walk towards him, her stunning body swaying beneath her sarong in a way that made his throat dry.

She reached him and handed him another drink. 'What was that all about?'

'Just me bragging shamelessly on how lucky I am to have found you.'

She laughed. 'Yeah, about that. You might need to pull back on the gushing a bit. You're putting our friends off.'

He caught her around her waist, tugged her mask aside and kissed her thoroughly. 'I have no intention of pulling back. Anyone who dares to approach me will be told how wonderful and gorgeous my wife is.'

His pulse soared when her fingers caressed his collarbone. 'I love you, Narciso.'

'And I love that I've made you happy enough to keep you from sleepwalking lately.'

'That reminder just lost you one brownie point.'

He pulled her closer. 'Tell me how to win it back, *per favore*,' he whispered fervently against her lips.

'Dance with me. And never stop telling me how much you love me.'

'For as long as I live, you'll know it, *amante*. That is my promise to you.'

* * * * *

A sneaky peek at next month...

MODERN™

POWER, PASSION AND IRRESISTIBLE TEMPTATION

My wish list for next month's titles...

In stores from 18th July 2014:

☐ Zarif's Convenient Queen – Lynne Graham

☐ His Forbidden Diamond – Susan Stephens

☐ The Argentinian's Demand – Cathy Williams

☐ The Ultimate Seduction – Dani Collins

In stores from 1st August 2014:

☐ Uncovering Her Nine Month Secret – Jennie Lucas

☐ Undone by the Sultan's Touch – Caitlin Crews

☐ Taming the Notorious Sicilian – Michelle Smart

☐ His by Design – Dani Wade

Available at WHSmith, Tesco, Asda, Eason, Amazon and Apple

Just can't wait?

Visit us Online

You can buy our books online a month before they hit the shops! **www.millsandboon.co.uk**

0714/01